MW00638394

Sons of the Rapture merges Kerouac, Faulkner, and O'Connor into a unique blend that speaks for young Southern folk coming of age nearly 150 years after the end of The Sin. You'll find yourself reading for the sound of the sentences as Dills creates characters with voices that scream from the void. This is an assured debut, and I hope Dills never goes quiet. —**DANIEL BUCKMAN**, author *Morning Dark, The Names of Rivers, Water in Darkness*

Todd Dills writes of culture-war veterans from street level, where the line dividing red from blue isn't drawn along state borders but zigzags between neighborhoods, houses, and bedrooms. In their attempt to survive battles someone else started, these characters speed through edged-out euphoria, then crash into a slur of lost time. Dills surveys the South, Chicago, even the fruited plains as he delivers a state of the union address many will deny but none can refute. This is how we're living now, in a past that isn't past and a future breaking backward. Dills's talent makes it all tick, his accuracy rings the alarm. —**PAUL A. TOTH**, author *Fishnet, Fizz*

Sons of the Rapture is the literary equivalent of the Fourth of July—as technically inventive as it is truly intimate and heartfelt, this fiery novel draws upon the grand mythology of the Old Testament and the spirit of Faulkner's best work. It's powerful storytelling and a reconciliation of our shared conflicts and histories. —**JOE MENO**, author *Hairstyles of the Damned, Bluebirds Used to Croon in the Choir*

SONS OF THE RAPTURE

a novel by

TODD DILLS

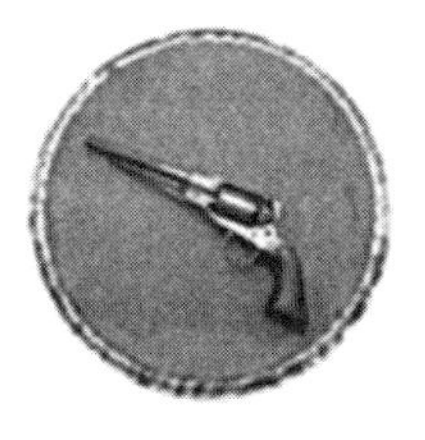

featherproof BOOKS

This is a work of fiction. All names, characters, places, and incidents are the product of the author's imagination. Where the names of actual celebrities or corporate entities appear, they are used for fictional purposes and do not constitute assertions of fact. Any resemblance to real events or persons, living or dead, is the product of *your* imagination.

Parts of this book have previously appeared in *Pindeldyboz, Kiss Machine,* and *The Tap.* Also, a small segment has been adapted and recorded for the *Radio Plays* audio zine.

Published by
featherproof books
Chicago, Illinois
www.featherproof.com

First Edition

10 9 8 7 6 5 4 3 2 1

Library of Congress Control Number: 2006923415

ISBN: 0-9771992-1-5
ISBN 13: 978-0-9771992-1-1

Set in Caslon

Printed in the United States of America

SONS OF THE RAPTURE

for the memory of

Carl E. and Catherine Bowers Long

of Silverstreet, South Carolina

I

BLESSED IS HE WHO READS ALOUD THE WORDS OF THE PROPHECY, AND BLESSED ARE THOSE WHO HEAR, AND WHO KEEP WHAT IS WRITTEN THEREIN; FOR THE TIME IS NEAR.

Revelation to John 1:3, Revised Standard Edition

Billy

INDEPENDENCE DAY, 2001, MY HOME STATE FINALLY elected, under pressure from the NAACP and against the hollered wish of many an Upcountry booster hick, to remove the Dixie battle flag from atop the battered capitol building in Columbia. No small matter, the act seemed a slap in the face more than anything else. Way up at the crest of the dome, folks on the ground could hardly see it. It now stood atop a low monument right off Gervais Street at the main entrance to the State House grounds. I saw the national news coverage. The NAACP boys and girls and their white college-student supporters had come out in force for a celebration, but seeing the new spot where the stars and bars would fly, they wailed and slapped themselves on the sides of their heads, vowing to continue their piddling boycott of commerce in the state. The Gaffney and Spartanburg and Blacksburg rednecks, with their HERITAGE NOT HATE and BLACKS RUN signs in their hands, found themselves with cause to celebrate and let fly a jubilant cheer.

The near century-old senator Thorpe Storm himself, ever diplomatic, decamped from his D.C. digs and made a trip to the State House, where the television crews caught him saying, "It's a great compromise, one that twice respects the heritage of the great nig—, excuse me [Storm affecting a cough], African-Americans of the fine state of South Carolina, and pays tribute to our fallen ancestors. My father and all our forebears would be proud." And he hobbled off, two aides propping him up by his elbows.

But Thorpe Storm had neglected to weigh in on a greater issue. Albert Ledbetter, an old friend of my crazy father's, who'd been calling me daily for the past three months ever since my father gave him my number one drunken night, rang from my hometown in Carolina and told me sensible folks weren't griping about the flag. The bigger issue on this day was that of the state ban on payouts from poker machines. Folks had been cashing in on the machines for decades. Not just big-time vendors, either, but small two- and three-machine convenience store operations, or folks running parlors out of their homes. Indeed, the pervasive influence of the rigged contraptions on my Carolina convenience store experience left me feeling at their very mention already a little sentimental, nostalgic for another time. Their trademark bleeping and blooping had been the sound track to the adrenalin rush attendant to many an adolescent petty theft caper. But I laughed, too, when Albert said the sensible, conscientious people of the great revolutionary state saw the ban as a fascist move on the part of the government, which was planning to institute an entirely state-run lottery. Said lottery was somehow bolstered by the idiotic antigambling morality of the Bible toters; if the lottery ain't gambling, Albert said, he didn't know what was. Seems the church folks couldn't jibe their high-toned ideals with the image of men and women smoking cigarettes in a convenience store in front of a noisy arcade game. Albert was mad, I say, himself tending toward the libertarian in ideology. But at once he told me a tale of good fortune, how his buddy Tope Talbert hustled up a great deal of work running the poker machines (their physical presence within the state's borders got banned as well) up to North Carolina in a big box truck he'd managed to commandeer for the week preceding. I went out and bought a copy of the *Chicago Tribune*, clipped a tiny article buried in its interior "Nation" section among hosts of fluffy previews of July the Fourth festivities, placing it in the top drawer of my dresser, where lay sundry items, mementos of other times I'd collected over the years. Here was my motley Confederate graycoat, found miraculously in an abandoned mill when I was a boy. Here were photos from a booth at the Two-Way of myself and my ex-lover Elsa, a bullet from a .22, a shot of Albert Ledbetter in a flannel shirt in front of my childhood home, can of beer in his hand and his hair long, wild, but receding from his forehead. I must have been ten years old when I took it.

Eventually, Albert the old man called back to ask me how I was doing. I didn't know what to tell him. My current girlfriend Sofie was off with her family in Germany. I didn't know whether she was coming back or not. We'd had a huge fight after I got drunk and puked in the drawer I'd offered her for her few possessions. I didn't know what I would do if she didn't return. I could barely afford my Chicago abode without her, which is to say nothing of love, of high feelings. But it's true my thoughts of late had turned toward women far more affecting than the German. I hadn't heard from the main, Elsa, in two years. Before she got up and fled Chicago, I caught her cavorting with a lesbian, or rather she came out and told me it was going on, which made it all even worse. I freaked. I trudged around town for a week with my teeth clenched against an inert rage. Elsa fled to her childhood home in France a month or so later, her sister Katje following, typically—fled Chicago like the cannibal Huguenots did St. Helena island in colonial times, losing their goddamned heads to the sea. Elsa lost her own to the sky, in an airplane. My friend Artichoke Heart says too much time separated from the ground breeds a fountain of false pride and contempt.

Two more weeks of clenched teeth, feeling smaller by the minute, I went to see Artichoke Heart. He stood wrapped in bright blue sweats in his building's courtyard with his brothers Charlie and Red, shooting a soccer ball through that bottomless metal trash can tacked somehow to the building's brick. I banged through the front gate, and A.H. gave a grin, puffed his distended trumpeter's cheeks. I grimaced at the spectacle.

Charlie lifted himself into the air, twirled, and dunked the soccer ball with a great metallic rattling into the can.

"Nice moves," I said.

A.H. dragged me by my graycoat's collar into the foyer, stopping, turning to me. With that curiously faggy lilt in his voice, he said, "Truth is, the thing with you and Elsa, her lesbian, it don't matter whatever. We're monkeys," he said.

"Right," I said. "But that changes nothing. Actually, we're absolutely *not* monkeys!" I flared, briefly, clenched my teeth and winced at the roots' tenderness. "I don't have the energy for this. Let me in," I said. He pushed me through the inner doorway. I fell into the recliner in his den. Then Artichoke Heart stood in the center of the room all slit-eyed and sarcastic, hair slicked back in that silly black pompadour atop his head, his fists planted on his hips. "Girl on boy. Girl on girl. Boy on boy. No difference whatever."

"Shit," I said. I introduced A.H. to one of my buddies up from the South Carolina hills for his vacation. I never missed the opportunity to scare the shit out of the people, when they came. "Good God Almighty!" he said, laying eyes on A.H. "Looks like a damned Alabama cotton nigger turned city queer!" Artichoke Heart you talk about in the third person even when he stands next to you. His eyes are slow-roving, deep brown, when he's not wearing the mirrored aviator sunglasses that force you to stare into yourself when you're with him; his air is hype, an outrageous rumor you can't quite believe; he's a sarcastic smartypants too, reads like an industrious college boy. Once upon a time, I could keep up.

"There's a writer, Bill," he said. "Russian. 'In the monkey economy,' the man says, to give you a bit of an explanation, 'insults aimed at us can always be jotted down,'" index finger of his right hand going quick to his temple, eyes catching mine in a splash. "And so something like this is a bare blast of nothing more than personal pride, I think. Brings out your competitive side." He took off his sweatshirt. I gazed out the window at Charlie and Red. The basket was hung just above the window, the soccer ball flew down from above again and again. I wondered how they'd got it up there, contemplated brick nails, screws, but my mind ran back to Elsa and the defeat, the low rage that burned up over a thing that should bother neither man nor woman. But my mind is a spaghetti strainer over a bonfire, a plastic thing warping in the heat, dumb and prefabricated. It does not take much lightly. Would that the drama flew on by without too much fanfare. I'd prefer such, I think, but if I was the near opposite of my crazy father Johnny Jones, in some respects we were identical. There in A.H.'s easy chair, staring into the courtyard (shadow of the soccer ball swinging and swinging down), I snapped my fingers with utter impatience, waiting for A.H. to change.

"You ready?" he said, after a time. He stood before me: red vinyl jumpsuit, insulated, I knew, for protection against the cold; around his neck a leather strap bringing to mind at once punk rock, high rodeo, and some sort of S&M thing; and as always, the tiara. It's aluminum, red, sculpted to the shape of flames that extend from the top of his head maybe eight inches. He has to stoop his way through doors, around ceiling fans. His natural habitat is a tavern with high ceilings, a ballroom, a magnificent cave.

He peered down to me, those roving eyes catching mine dead-on for a fraction of a second before roving on. He moved for the door.

"She slept with a girl, man," I said, the now-old hot feeling of the truth and the lie at once welling up behind my breastbone.

He sat on the coffee table across from me, shook his head like to reprimand me. "You do it all the time, don't you?"

I rose from the chair, standing up above him like my 5'7" was challenge enough.

"It's competition, see," he said. "Dumb, not sane. You can't possibly compete with a girl when a girl is the prize." He stood, pushing me back down into the chair.

"So typical, you shit. Help me. I'm fighting…" I threw up my hands and closed my eyes, head falling back. "Billy," A.H. said, sitting down again and waving that finger like a prohibitive mother. "Beauty is that which is approachable. Beauty is innocence gone bad, viewed from a high tower. Beauty is—" he paused. He stood tall again, way up there in the air. "Three years and you'll be checking your e-mail. You'll get a message from her. She'll be talking about her new man. You'll return the letter, and you'll still be in love with her. And you'll tell her about your girlfriend, and she'll say she's still in love with you, too. Or maybe it won't be told, but you'll know." He turned and walked to the kitchen. I started to say something. "Save it," he hollered. I closed my eyes, fought to retain some sort of composure. I breathed. When I opened my eyes A.H. was sitting again in front of me. He held a frozen peach, tossed it into the air a few times, eyes roving to the ceiling and back to his hand. It was part of the winter stash his sweet old mother would overnight him from South Carolina every summer. He stood, motioned for me to follow outside. Red and Charlie still jumped, twirled, shot, their mouths wide and breathing crystal clouds into the cold. "To Johnny's," A.H. said to me, brushing his brothers back. He jumped, dunked the peach into the tacked-up trash can.

"What the hell was that for?" I said.

A.H. picked the peach from the frozen ground and dunked it again. Red and Charlie waddled backward, mouths agape. Charlie told him he was crazy, but A.H. had fixed his gaze on me. "Hear that sound?" he said. He dropped the peach, which fell to the snow, the ice, made less sound than a cracking pop-top. "That's how small all of this is," he said.

I put my face in my hands and mock-howled in pain.

"Now, I'm willing to listen," he said. "To Johnny's."

It never mattered that Artichoke Heart knew everything there was to know about me. At Johnny's Grill, a little diner around the corner, we talked often. It helped me sort. This day would be no different.

ARTICHOKE HEART WAS A SOUTH CAROLINA JONES, same as me: Jones, William Harmony. Eventually he left Chicago too, got up his courage and boarded a plane headed south—he never flew on planes, normally, hadn't left Chicago for ten years, he told me the day I met him. Same day I met Elsa, actually. A.H. played west-side food fests, "tastes" of this and that. He took the stage decked out in sequined cowboy vests, hair done up in a greasy pompadour, and played wanky, old-fashioned Mexican norteño with the crew of his four brothers, the Joneses. That fateful summer people were bouncing in the streets like not since seen. The boys revitalized the west-side block party scene. It wasn't my bag, though I'd admit he was good, if asked. He put on an ecstatic show.

Taste of Kedzie, at the square down the block from my apartment, sticks in my mind as a half-assed gathering of lonely apartment hounds, where one was lucky to catch the GN'R tribute band that used to play around the neighborhood, unlucky if ending the day tired and bored with, at most, four other showgoers out on the street, hearing one of four different combos, all the same, very pandering in their instrumentation and obvious attempt at PC. Black singer, male. White longhair bassist rocking on his heels behind a big butch of a lady drummer, also white. There may be a black female or Latina keyboardist, but always the male Latino trumpeter up front, squeaking monotonously away: "La Bamba," "Black Magic Woman," "You Are the Sunshine of My Life," "Black Dog," they played it all, though the humdrum affairs always paled to that first one I witnessed—featuring none other than one Artichoke Heart, the new in block party entertainment.

I was only out for a quick coffee at a square cafe, though I carried my chrome flask as always, just in case. But stepping off my block I eyed a monstrous vinyl sign stretched across the facing buildings the other side of the square, satanic red lettering announcing today's performer: ARTICHOKE HEART. The square jammed full of bodies, yellow food tents stewed, crawled with souls. I looked around for someone I knew—vaguely recognized, rather, for I'd been in Chicago just shy of two months—and found no one but anonymous Spanish speakers, an ugly white man or two with an uglier woman draped over his shoulder.

When I spotted her she was wading through this crowd: Elsa, a goddess with piano-key fingers wrapped tight around a stick on which was speared a rounded specimen of gyro meat. She was followed by her tall, functionally Amazonian equivalent: sister Katje, I would learn. The beautiful sight instilled a quality of bravery in my bones it's likely I should not have felt. I shot through a couple and grabbed her by the wrist. She yelped in protest, whirled around and caught an old woman in the side of the head with a freewheeling elbow. I laughed, genuine hilarity bubbling up in my body. The girl muttered apologies to the old lady, then cocked a hip, staring down the plane of her nose in a squint. "Have a dime, dear woman?" I said, a shudder passing through the loose flesh of my premature Jones jowls. She didn't say anything for a moment. "Jesus hell," I muttered, and made like to turn away, but she stopped me, baring her crooked teeth in a sly grin, knowing too well my gambit. "I'm Elsa," she said, extending her ghostly white arm, hand out, which I took. She chomped down on the tube of meat. "This is my sister Katje," she went on, shredded bits popping half-chewed from her mouth. I proffered my flask only after a long pull for myself. Her dark eyes went wide. Katje squeezed up behind her, laid her chin on her sister's shoulder and grimaced at the sun. "How do you do?" she said.

I felt even surlier then, like a cowboy or something in my T-shirt and jeans in front of the two pristine women. I introduced myself with a twang as "SC Bill." The ladies rolled their eyes, passed the flask between themselves. A wild gust of wind then kicked up, sending a ripple through the crowded square, a keen murmur rising as heads turned toward the stage. We gazed with the crowd up there, *and lo,* there was Artichoke Heart. "Wow," the lady Elsa said in appraisal. I took the flask from her and pulled hard, exhaled at the terminus to the sight of the all-Jones crew of bass, drums, guitar, accordion, and just by the front microphone A.H.'s silvery trumpet resting quietly on a stand. Artichoke Heart bent at the waist to prize the instrument; the flames on his tiara aimed out at the crowd. A dust cloud rose and hung in the now windless sky above us. A hush fell over the assembled. Elsa worked at the belly of her T-shirt, raised up on her tiptoes. "Look at the guy!" she said. A man at my left raised his fist and bellowed happily in Spanish. And without a word A.H. and his band bounced through three polka numbers, covered MC Hammer's "Can't Touch This." I clutched my own gyro tube by then and put out a hefty shout-out to my new friend. She pulled hard on both my flask and arm beside me, smiling into me, shouting "HOLY—JESUS—CHRIST—this guy is GOOD!" her face screwed up sweetly like she'd never been happier. I pretended I couldn't hear her, leaned closer, and fireworks sprung from A.H.'s stage, the final song another exotic, accordion-based number. I set my gaze there, lit a cigarette, and pulled the final bit from the flask. I noted the man's devilish tiara, cheeks distended as he blasted away, the quintet whee-wonk-wonking their way through some of the most beautifully crazed music I'd ever heard. Elsa blew smoke in my ear, saying something—it didn't matter what—and my mind flew high over the stage and square to where I could look down on it all, the small traffic circle, south end full of people, the bulbous yellow tops of the food tents and the smoke billowing out from their sides, the thick molasses stench of it all reaching way up here, opening up the sterile angles of the Chicago grid, the little blocks of neighborhoods, the right angles, the 45-degree angles of diagonal flow streets that connected them all, the fine curve of the expressway gray and desolate and jammed on its way downtown. It made some sense, for the moment. I could approach it.

WE HUNG AROUND THE SQUARE LONG AFTER THE show. We waddled arm in arm in arm to Johnny's Grill, which sits in a corner space on the square walled with glass on each street-facing side. The interior is cut in half by a diagonal counter, where we assumed a short row, recovering with coffee. I sat between the two and we told the generalities of our lives. They were new to the city, though not the States. Los Angeles for three years. New York for two. Elsa: a would-be painter, would-be for she'd migrated from college to college for five years with no more than four finished pieces to show for it. Katje: a customer servicer, primarily, a phone pumper with vague pretensions to the written word. "Though I've been dogged on the heels of this one for these five years," she said, which I took to suggest a complacency similar to her sister's. Elsa smiled at the pronouncement. I pictured Katje stooped, shuffling her massive feet along a sidewalk behind a jumping, prancing Elsa. "And you?" Katje asked me, her sister nodding to reiterate.

I gazed out the window. What had I to tell them? "I've been here for two months. Solid. Got real bored in Carolina when all my college buddies got married. So I left. My job stinks. I've got a problem with my back that won't go away."

"It's where?" Elsa asked, which brought me back to the beautiful specter before me. I swiveled to turn to Elsa's long hands, which went to work on my back. Katje rose for the restroom. I started to tell Elsa of South Carolina, amping the grotesquery: "My friend Eric's got a brother who lost his penis in the gulf war when a lady nurse he was doing behind a sandy embankment turned out to be an Iraqi operative." My head bobbed in the truth and the lie at one in my tale. Eric was a veteran of that war and had called me a few days before to tell me he had dick cancer.

Elsa only chuckled, now kneading my shoulders. Katje came back and sat on the far side of her sister, who told a story about time she spent shooting documentary footage with a British filmmaker while living among Burmese resistance fighters. I was a little floored.

"Yep," I said, now opting for the simple truth. "My brother Bobby's 25 at this point and's been in jail since he was 17." For the killing of my and his own mother, he sat now in an SC penitentiary receiving periodic visits from Albert Ledbetter, whom my father paid for the task. I didn't give them the full detail: we talked only general absurdity, a thing I'd found easy to do, something people could enjoy in the great city. Can you tell a good tasteless joke to get us through the discomfort of being around our fellow humans? We'll make you the goddamned mayor.

And all the while, fireworks burst from those long fingers on my back, the French femme a veritable expert. She started talking about my favorite band at the time, Rocket From the Crypt, whom she'd met briefly back in LA, and I knew we were on.

Four refills into our sit here, Artichoke Heart strode into the space bedecked in street clothes, apparently. In full red jumpsuit, tiara, greasy Elvis hairdo, the man was followed by a cavalcade of admirers, brown-faced boys with baggy T-shirts half-tucked into jeans that sagged around their butts. Johnny's Grill's proprietor, Dean, came swinging feet-first over an empty space at the counter to fend the boys off. They sidled backward, waving their arms in parody of their future selves. A.H. smiled at them, taking the seat next to me, and Dean poured him a coffee like it was nothing, like he knew the man. And he did. "Wow!" Elsa whispered.

She really liked saying that. I got a little nervous in the man's presence myself. I trained my sight on Dean, who was back behind the counter by now tapping a syncopated beat with a metal spatula on the flattop cooker. "He's so—" Elsa pausing, then whispering on. "So cool! Look at him!"

I turned to A.H., now determined in spite of my minor trepidation to show the girls something of myself. "Bill. Nice to meet you," I said, thrusting my hand out like I might have been a vacuum-cleaner salesman, awkwardly holding it there not grasped in the space between myself and the red-vinyl-clad man.

A.H. only nodded, his deep voice then booming above the precious silence left in the terminus of Dean's syncopated tapping. "Good to meet you, Bill," he aped back, just barely letting his eyes catch mine before turning back to his coffee.

I asked him his name. He took a long, slow sip, put the cup down and exhaled dramatically. "Artichoke Heart," he breathed, distending his cheeks after a long inhale.

"Oh, I meant your real one," I said.

His eyes then went wide, caught mine for a long moment. He chuckled. Elsa and Katje gaped around my shoulder, their hot breath falling over my neck. The whites of the man's eyes grew further at the women's grinning faces before he pulled from a chest pocket in his jumpsuit his mirrored aviator shades, slipping them across his nose to dim the sight. "Jones," he said, proffering his hand to me and prompting a series of guffaws from the women. "Artichoke Heart Jones."

And we hung around all afternoon, told stories, and ended the day at a bar down the road. The pure chance of our time did matter, for the fun was had, and a beautiful trap was set for each of us. Thereafter we traveled in a pack. A.H. took the point, Elsa and I groping each other just behind him with Katje at our backs to ward off opportunistic assholes, those who would attempt to upset the delicate balance we made. We convoyed to parties, drank in corners, joked, and got along quite fabulously. A few months into it, I got fired from my job at a downtown bakery, and Johnny's Grill was where me and A.H. met in the aftermath. I told him I'd been stealing from the register, it was true, and probably deserved what I got. "No problem," A.H. said, "though that will be on your 'record.' We want to say you don't even have one." So he set me up with a guy he knew in the Illinois Division of Waste Management,

Frank Christ—"Tell him I sent you," A.H. said—who apparently owed A.H. a favor. I didn't ask him for particulars, and when I finally got a haircut and met with the man, when I told Mr. Christ who sent me, the old man's brow lost its wrinkled consternation and I got the job.

A time of bliss ensued with Elsa on my twin bed. The apartment took on the smell of her perfume and sex, and she talked my ears off while atop my stomach. I loved her there, above me, chatting with abandon about my dark eyes, goofball humor. She began to give me the rundown of her previous men, an African named Aime, Hugo the Portuguese, Yves back home. She toppled down the uncertain hills of her memory and I dogged behind her like Katje—Dutch, I learned, adopted. My heart fluttered anxiously, elated, occasionally bored though I was, at the spoken history of the lady. At bottom Elsa's voice is a salve for your wounds, sexy like cold water. But her past began to loom in my mind like charging Confederates flanked by outrageous artillery. I could take Elsa's monologues no longer and told her about it, laid it out hard that I did not under any circumstances want to hear about her men past.

"Jealous, jealous man!" she cried, laughing wildly from her perch on my stomach and digging her fingers into my ribs. "Jealous of the past!"

I did not laugh. I spent the night grinding my teeth while I slept.

I ran to A.H., who told me how full of shit I was, how Elsa would see that just fine, too. Johnny's Grill was enveloped in ice that brutal Chicago winter. The wagging lips of the old men scattered around the counter like to have frozen even poised above their coffee mugs. A.H. perched on his haunches atop the counter and gave a sermon about my plight to the men. Now what will this Billy boy do?

One of the old fools remarked that the only way to control a woman was to beat the evil out of her.

The next day, A.H. played banjo and guitar for me in his little den. We went on to Johnny's, and he listened to the whole again in front of Dean, the proprietor, who laughed and said I sounded like a bitch in heat without a mind or even a dong to act on it. The men around the counter joined him in his cold laughing.

I smoked more and more laid up on my bed, evenings. Elsa assumed her customary spot on top of me, talking. I blew smoke in her eyes if she leaned too close, even burned the tips of her bangs once or twice—half-hearted accidents. The rotten, acrid smell of burning hair filled the apartment.

One morning, after an unpleasant dream that involved Elsa and out-of-work porn actors, I woke sweating and crying. I did not want to hear the same shit from A.H. again, so I hooked up with Dean at Johnny's on my own. He took me to his Serbian uncle's place outside Milwaukee. I shot and killed a raccoon with a little .22, a fine shot, Dean said. He skinned the beast, cleaned it, giving me the mangled bullet to commemorate the day. Then he cooked it in his patented (or so I was told) raccoon stew. We ate it. The meat tasted like the smell of burning hair, if that makes sense. "Raccoons are crazy little fuckers, rodents," Dean said, his fork pulling at the gristle in his plastic bowl.

"You cook a mean one," I forced out, washing yet another acrid mouthful down with a pull from my beer. A strong urge to spit didn't subside for weeks.

After two days absence, I returned home to find Elsa in my apartment, smiling in front of some TV rerun like I'd never been gone. I told her I'd been called home by my father, my brother had died in prison and the funeral was just yesterday. She brushed the lie off, mostly, beckoned me to the bed and made love to me as I smoked cigarette after cigarette to keep from spitting, crying into the stench of her burned hair, the memory of the taste of the wayward rodent crowding my senses so that I gagged at every pull of the cigarette, Elsa giggling, screaming at the pleasure of it.

I left the apartment after, cruised the alleyways with the .22 I'd stolen from Dean's uncle. I liked the feel of it tucked at the small of my back, though I worried that it would misfire and blow my ass off. The alleyway behind my place led me to the trash cans behind the square's restaurants, where I found an open bin crawling with rats. I stopped ten yards off, pulled the gun, kicked at the asphalt under my feet prompting a further swarm of vermin in every direction, behind and under the bins lining the alley or into the mindless safety of crevices under concrete steps. Some, certainly, only burrowed further into the filth. One mighty son of a bitch had the gall to sit stock still atop the mounds of garbage there; the thing stared straight into me, an opportunity too great to resist. My arms went numb as I took aim, fired, and the fucker flew over backward in the bin.

Next day, I woke up and called A.H. I told him Dean had taken me out to his uncle's and fed me the best damned food I'd ever had.

"Dean cook you a raccoon?" A.H. asked.

"How'd you know?"

Artichoke Heart didn't speak, but I could picture him on his end of the line, casually laid back in his big orange chair, wide cryptic grin spread across his face, the grin that told you he'd heard it all.

ELSA NEVER FIGURED THE LIE I TOLD HER, HARMLESS as it was considering her seemingly devil-may-care attitude toward our coupling. I did not tell her either of my nightly excursions through Chicago alleyways in search of the next kill. Three weeks in I'd laid off three more rats. The killing offset the pain, somehow. And I drank and drank to cover the guilt of the lies, the rage, everything, and it all seemed to be working. Then I left the gun at home, and our crew rolled over to a friend's party. Bunch of art school kids. Hundreds packed into the little kitchen and den areas of a third-floor two-bedroom. Drunk, everyone. The atmosphere was steamy with heat inside the place; frigid Chicago winter death ruled the outer climes. Me and Elsa parked on a couch by the front windows, and in a bright moment she thrust her hand down behind the belt of my leather pants, her fingers wrapped right around my privates. She pressed her body against mine, the passel of others in the room all huddled tight together on the improvised dance floor in front of us. I did what I felt in that close heat and drunk and got my hand in between our bodies and unzipped my jeans for more room. The noodlings of a saxophone rose like an atom bomb in the dark. My eyes snapped tightly closed.

And then above it all I hear this "Goddamn!"—Elsa's "Goddamn!" It's hysterically funny—high-pitched, breathy, French as all hell.

But when my shaft popped free, I felt a slap come hard across my face. Elsa gave a stiff pull at my nose with the same hand, zipped me up with the other. Then she jumped back and stood glaring like a redneck queen would at her cheating husband, one hip cocked and with a hand stuck hard just above its curve, eyes slit down to the black of the pupils. The other hand pointed and looped around as she told me off. Ten or so of the other partygoers formed tight flanks at her side like as backup. What was I gonna do to her? "Jesus hell," I muttered. I clamped and unclamped my lids a few times trying to really focus on the mutant circus: Elsa and Katje made up the point, the flanks decked out in shiny or goofy-striped shirts, more than a few pairs of tight pants with outrageous fur fringe at the cuffs, sunglasses there even in the dark. None of them liked me much: I'd pissed off too many during drunken blackouts when I finally spoke my mind to the trust-funded crew. Thing is, I could control this crowd, if I really thought on it: I pulled my aviators from my shirt pocket and slid them slow across my nose, nodding a little as the whole place erupted in laughter.

We left soon after. As if in spite of my little victory the eruption had thrown a gigantic roadblock between various possible one-night stands groping along; the place felt dead as a bar mitzvah or something. I wore my aviators behind A.H. on a cold and dark walk to the Two-Way, a place with two entrances, an old oak bar, and a pervasive air of sexual ambivalence. We crowded into a booth by the bar as the old Chicago drunks sat above us flinging bad jokes and groans around the counter. Elsa fumed a little about the party incident. "I can't believe you fucking took your cock out!" though she was laughing, too. Katje and A.H. just rolled their eyes from across the table as finally I took off my aviators and stared at Elsa's mouth. I was drunk.

A few more drinks and we're all stuck listening to A.H. talk about his experiments with dudes, appropriately enough, considering the environs. In full regalia, tiara and all like it'd been stuck to his skin, he clung to the glory of his minor fame; consequently he was a favorite at bars such as this one, where the old Chicago drunks and hipsters formed a cohort. "Bill," he said. "You've never stuck your cock up a fella's ass?" And he grinned that sweaty, sarcastic thing. Elsa and her sister broke into laughter so high-pitched and loud that I quickly wiped the disgusted look from my face with the back of a hand.

"Well," I said, simply.

"You haven't." A.H. nodded as if to confirm the truth of his statement.

"Oh no…" wide-eyed, me. I motioned to the bartender for more drinks. Three burly drunks at the counter were visibly tuned into our conversation. A.H. went on about how he'd once taken on three faggot ex-cons at once. The three, he said, were friends of his brother Charlie. Visions of pedophiles in riot gear flooded my senses—Charlie was at least ten years A.H.'s junior. A.H. laughed long and loud, nodding to my disgusted expression. "The guy," he said, looking to Elsa. "He wouldn't know beauty if it walked up and said hello."

I was now very drunk. The bartender laid our beers on the edge of the bar. I reached up quick, grabbing mine and sucking hard on it.

"He knows me," said Elsa, and they all laughed. I sucked down my perturbation, the lot of them staring like they expected me to vomit. I might. What kind of conversation was this? What a thing to push on a man so obviously tanked, uncomfortable, sitting here with his goddamned ladyfriend. But I wasn't so drunk I couldn't think, for I then pulled a kernel out of that sentiment, as my friends continued to talk, figuring I'd play the game a bit. "Now the question!" I hollered. "It's what does the lady Betty think of all this?" I was positively beaming here, understand, as A.H. began to sneer. Artichoke Heart's sometime girlfriend Betty was a homey south-sider with an old maid's hairdo and, a little like A.H. himself, a dictionary's worth of words to say—no, to yell—about everything.

"Does she know, for instance, about the three pedophiles in their riot gear?" I leaned way back in the booth, smiling, letting it all sink in. But A.H. remained calm.

"Who said anything about riot gear?" Elsa said, but I kept my gaze fixed on the man in front of me, who smiled like he'd read my mind. And maybe he had. "Not quite sure," he said. "You know, I don't think Betty knows." And he laughed yet again, a big belly-laugh, his head falling back from our booth; it was forced, I knew. The boys at the bar bought it, though, guffawing and reaching around each other to slap the black man A.H. on the back like he was an old pal. They all bought it. Elsa and Katje chuckled their ways through a sip each, and A.H. adjusted his tiara to cap it, pushing the thing farther up atop his head. He winked at me as the crowd laughed on.

"Well you should fucking tell her," I said.

"It was a long time ago," he said. "Fun while it lasted, but the ladies are much more the thing that gets me going." A.H. looked toward Elsa and Katje and winked some more.

"But what if you told her, see?" I said. "I think you know damned well what would happen."

Then Elsa grabbed my shoulder and turned my drunken body to her. "Women are not so," she said, pausing, "so prudish about it? That right?" Her voice cut up in pitch and volume like that of a stepped-on cat.

"Shit," I said.

A.H. cocked his head and drove home the point. "The opposite's opposite," he said. "It's impossible to compete with a girl. In the case of a dude. Or vice-versa."

"Right," Elsa said. But I was fucking lost. I set my sights on the dudes at the bar, who now were giving drooling, gape-mouthed sorts of looks at A.H.

Elsa's wild howl brought me back after a time to the picture of Katje smiling sarcastically at me. "Fucking what?" I said.

A.H. chuckled. "The man's got a point."

"Who's got a point?" I said.

"You do."

"I didn't say shit."

Then Elsa sat up, rolled her beautifully bulbous eyes down to me. "What would you say, for instance, if you knew I'd had a girlfriend?" I didn't say a word for a long moment, was aware only vaguely of a slight sinking feeling in my gut. I managed to stammer "And had you?" which she answered with a nod, a shrug of her shoulders and "There was a girl at the party wearing a beret. That's her."

"What?" I stammered, but she was smiling at me, that smile to die for: lips parted just a little like an opening flower, a sexy lilt to one side of her mouth. And with that smile the knowledge of her pronouncement sank in. "Fucking outrageous," I said, turning back to the bar, the old men just laughing away with themselves. I pointed. "What the fuck are you laughing at?" I said.

Artichoke Heart tried to deflate the uneasiness in the air between us by ordering a round of shots, then another, and another, which more or less worked. I donned my aviators after the fourth round and had forgotten about most everything. I rose, swaying, to go to the bathroom and was collared by one of the old guys as I passed the bar. He swung my drunken body onto a stool too close to him for my comfort. "What's the word, my man?" he said.

"The word is my fucking head hurts, friend," I said, and I stuck my pointer finger then an inch from his nose, curled it in, and "BOOM!" I said, with thoughts of rats braver and uglier than even he, whose eyes shot wide before he laughed. "Ever shot a rat?" I hollered.

He got up from his chair.

"It's an amazing thing," I said. "You look into the fucker's eyes before it dies and you know what you see? It knows. In this city, these rats know what a gun pointed at their heads means. So what's the answer, friend?" He shuffled back and away. I stood and stepped toward him slowly, backing him up against the pool table. "You done it yourself? You look like you might, I'll say." The man's jeans were smeared with grease, his coat a dastardly, stinking thing. He nearly collapsed backward onto the table. I took one more step forward before being spun around by the hard hand of Artichoke Heart, who stood there in his sunglasses, near identical to my own. "Let's go," he said. I stared at my reflection in his shades for a full minute, it seemed, the crowd gathered around us staring, gawking, unsure even of its own existence at this moment. We'd given them a show. A.H. could keep this up indefinitely. A bright bulb hung just over our heads on the end of a wire. I closed my eyes. When I opened them he was still there. As was I, there in his sunglasses, I thought, and it broke me. I turned away, remembered the man and pool table behind me. "Wait a second," I said, shaking out a blooming pain in my head. I turned around and, of course, met only the enraged gazes of not only the current billiards players but every shithead who waited his turn. "Shit hell," I said, and we left, wading through the gawking circle of hipsters, the old men on the other side of them, a few of the latter vowing that we'd never see the interior of the Two-Way again. But we exited through the north door, and the entryway through the south would be forever open to us, as it later turned out.

Elsa and Katje stood in the cold outdoors, looked at me like I might kill them before I said, "Come on ladies." Only you will save us.

I lurched home with Elsa, stopping once to piss in an alleyway, and reached the door to my place to choke at the smell of burned hair that crept through the gaps, then hitting the hot interior and bursting into a fit of coughing so violent I thought I might vomit. I stewed. Elsa made straight for the bathroom. I prized the .22 from its spot in my underwear drawer. She came back out and sat down. She asked about her girlfriend. I didn't speak. She told me that when she'd made her confession, I looked like someone had punched me in the nose. "What would you do if I told you some shit like that?" I asked, unable to smile or frown or even summon the muscles I would need to put on an expression appropriate for a man asking a question. I stood by the doorway and swayed. She hadn't an answer for me and started to cry a little. "I've got to walk," I said, and left the place. There was a police car by the restaurant garbage bins, a cop sitting idly in wait for a man with a gun. I ambled on by, rats hopping at my feet.

Four blocks down I made the mistake of spending the last bullet on a beast as it trundled in the open air down the alley in flight from me. I was stumbling along and missed every shot, had to duck a police siren I could only hear, at some remove behind me, wailing through the whine of the city. I ran the alleys and emerged onto a street nearly a mile east of my apartment, gasping. I could see the freeway from this spot, the lights of cars falling around a turn toward unknown fates. I watched them for a time, the siren wailing in diminuendo behind me before it fell off completely. I thought nothing, felt for the gun at my back. It was there. I sat and must have for hours, or I sat there for days, maybe, as the next weeks were only a stasis of teeth-grinding and clenched fists.

Elsa and Katje had in truth been planning a departure for a long time, so it shouldn't have been much of a surprise that they left those weeks on. They'd said they'd be coming back, before all this, but I knew it was over. After they escaped, I was so broken I took to carrying the gun at all times, empty though it was, and I did not use it. I floated along.

ARTICHOKE HEART HAD A GOOD PIECE TO SAY ON IT at Johnny's Grill those weeks later, myself recasting every particular for the man, even his own part in the conflagration, which had the effect of making him start and pull his aviators from his nose as if he'd forgotten something about himself and needed more light to see it. Finally, he removed the sunglasses entirely, I removed mine, and once the bulk of the rehashing was done we talked about notions of beauty, a useless and stupid thing for two men to be talking about, I thought. A.H. didn't say much new.

"Well," I said.

"Well indeed," said he.

"Now she was fucking beautiful," I said, of Elsa. Dean heard, jumping atop the counter and spreading his arms like a bear, screaming the proclamation to the rest of the diner. All the old men bellowed regrets: what a goddamned shame. At least A.H. is a good ear, in spite of the three hoops he wears in each of his own.

"There's two ways to deal," he said, there at the window counter with a view of the square, the stone Nazi eagle atop the monument in the center. The sun beamed in, reflecting in a steady, blinding glare off A.H.'s red jumpsuit. "The first is tried and true, however crass it may seem. And that's the simple fact that the only cure for a woman is another one."

"What wise son of a bitch told you that?"

A.H. ignored me. I swiveled and made a gesture of corroboration at Dean, who tipped his ludicrous chef's hat. "My uncle's looking for his gun," he said. A.H. had donned his aviators again, but his eyebrows could be made out above the frames, raised high at Dean's statement. I stood, pulling the piece from my belt, walked to the counter, and laid it down. Dean smiled as the old men gawked and settled into their stools with a little more respect, I imagine, for my short frame.

"Damn," A.H. said.

"You ever kill a rat?"

"Well yes," he said, "though not quite literally a rat."

"It can be quite a rewarding experience," I said.

He ignored me, seemed lost in thought, distractedly putting his sunglasses back on his face once, twice, and again before allowing them to sit firmly on his nose. And then he turned, and I caught a flash of my stooped figure in the mirrors before I turned my own gaze to the square. "Your second option," he said. "You sit back and you chew on it. You live. Turns out ten years later you're 40 or however old and you're still chewing, alone, a full set of dentures or crowns or whatever."

Out by the Nazi eagle an old man and a dog collaborated on a snowman, the dog yapping and hopping up and down fluffing snow in arcs from the ground and onto the base snowball, onto which the old man heaved the next ball and now backed away.

A.H. went on, "And somewhere in the space between those two opposites is the beauty. Somewhere in there you're able to pull your sentiment out and examine it, to operate there as a unit unencumbered by the limits of your own mind." Almost offhandedly he put this shit out there. I hardly even remembered the first thing, though I perked at the last, glanced over at my funhouse reflection in his glasses. My hair was big, curly and wild. I stared back at myself as a clown with bubble lips and a black peacoat. I tried in vain to sense the eyes behind the man's lenses. "You tend toward destruction," he said. "It's like that's all you can do, sometimes." On the square's snowcap man and beast were at one and the snowman now wrecked, the man on his back and cackling as the dog stood on the man's stomach and licked his face.

I let A.H. in on the way I couldn't talk to Elsa for a week after that night, the pounding, the gnashing of teeth and the killing, how it was the only thing I could do to get me thinking practical, strategizing about something other than her, and how she should have hated me, but she simply did not, how she was at least a decent person, yes, and I couldn't bear her being so—how she couldn't wake me as I gnashed on, waking only after hours and my mouth feeling like a muscle-bound dwarf had been cracking my molars with a mini tire iron. I let A.H. in on what I'd thought, standing and watching the expressway traffic blow through the cold night: that, after all, I would miss her when she was gone, terribly. I'd be sick. "But I did not do anything," I said, to stop the flight.

Then I told my friend about the '73 Nova I'd put an old Chrysler Hemi into, back in SC. He said he'd heard that one. Then: where was it now?

Artichoke Heart could appreciate struggle and misfortune, the way your general human has an eye for scandal, or for fine automobiles.

"Me and my buddy Eric were drunk. There's a main drag where I grew up—"

"Cherry Road," A.H. said. "It's the only memorable thing in town, really."

"—Friday nights the races started at the K-Mart and Wal-Mart parking lots, where the one gang of rednecks would sit on one side of the road in the K lot, and the other gang, the prissier versions of the folks across the street, people with rich fathers but a comparable amount of would-be shitkicking tendency, they'd hang out in the competing Wal-Mart's lot. Me and Eric didn't particularly belong to either crowd. We were car enthusiasts, solely. Kids, at that."

"I know the type. You," A.H. now pointing at my chest. "Yes, you," he said, "but you've got a little shitkicker in there too."

"Sometimes to get a little fun out of anything you gotta get your hands in the mud," I said, which maybe my crazy father told me once.

"There you go again," he said.

I spoke as loud as I could manage. "Fuck you. We hung out there some Saturday nights, and we'd race the hell out of them. After I put in the Hemi, couldn't nobody take me, mostly. Eric had a 1968 Camaro and wasn't any less of a force himself. One particular night there was this guy out there with a goat."

"A goat?"

"A GTO. Big green one. To this day I got no clue what he had under the hood, but it had to be some sort of custom job. Beat the hell out of me. Eric was in the car with me the first time, so I asked him to get out on the far and gone chance it was his fat ass, bless the man, the extra weight, you know, that was holding me up. Of course Eric would not have it for me to be beat, so he got out. In the K-Mart parking lot where the no-sass-or-priss shitkickers were. And he started raising hell at the boy with the goat. Talking alcohol, surely, but I wasn't so far behind him. I walked over to the guy and insisted that we take it down Cherry again, though it was well past racing time, getting on 5AM, and most of the shitkickers were heading home, redneck queens on their heels."

"Queens?" A.H. said.

"In a manner of speaking," I said. "I meant women. The guy actually declined a few times. I figured he'd be hell-bent on whipping me again, especially considering how bad he'd beat me before—got down past the mall before I'd even hit the third light. He had the look too, you know: the thin, peach-fuzz mustache, the spiked hair on top, curls along his neck."

"Mid-80s white man," A.H. said, and I told him how "I finally insisted that the guy was a pussy, didn't want to get embarrassed by me in front of his woman, who stood there beside him, hair frosted and crimped in shelves down her back. 'Whip his ass,' she said, and then it was on.

"And that's what I'm getting to," I said. "This girl totally ruled the guy. He wouldn't do a fucking thing until she pipes in and the death match is on. And what did he have? He had shit. He had a badass car, but what otherwise? Nothing. But the girl. And that's what I'm talking about. We'll do anything these women say—"

But A.H. was more interested in the car, so I told him how I lost control of it as the rear wheels spun up to 30 miles an hour and wrapped the beauty around a telephone pole off Cherry. "I take it you lost again," he said.

"Oh yes. Got out of the hospital a week later with a broken leg and not much more. Pretty damned lucky."

Then he took off his aviators and stared a hole through my head. I wouldn't see much more of him before he left. His band played a club or two the following spring, and I saw him there. But we didn't talk much. The streetfest scene died down. Chicago seemed to have had enough of Artichoke Heart. Or so he felt. My apartment filled up a little on account of him, though. When he fled, me and my new lady Sofie got a coffee table and a little blue chaise. By then I was cured of Elsa, yes. The New Year's Eve after she left I was sulking about at a party, totally wasted, and suddenly there's another tall European in my face, telling me I look sad and that she married a guy to stay in the States and ended up hating him. Divorced after a year's time. Well, I said. "Wait a second, where you from?" Her then-boyfriend caught us kissing in a back stairwell and came at me swinging. Busted my aviators all to pieces. But Sofie somehow thought it was valiant when I drunkenly beat the man within an inch of his life. Star-crossed, surely.

"We are fucking monkeys, I'm telling you," A.H. staring me down. I averted my eyes and looked out Johnny's windows and onto the square, empty now but for the cars and the half-finished snowman and snow and that hideous eagle.

"Hey Artichoke Heart!" Two youngish guys burst into Johnny's and saluted A.H., who nodded solemnly, flipping his aviators back up onto his nose, and I laughed till my eyes burst, tears flowing from my spot here and down along the floor, freezing just outside the door.

"That's a fact," A.H. said. "Monkeys." He laughed some himself. "You're a sight," he said.

"I am something," I said. I cried like a goddamned sissy when A.H. left this town. There was nothing I could think to say to anyone else, not even to Sofie. All my business dealt with just below the surface of my own skull, which was a headache, after all. But Artichoke Heart was a city boy to the core, and I always held the thought the trumpeter would make his way back to Chicago, searching out the dream, the crowds, and the drunks.

Albert

JOHNNY JONES, LATE-CENTURY HUSTLER, ROMANTIC soul undaunted by the technology in front of him, could not abide a certain scene from his boyhood. U.S. Senator Thorpe Storm meddled periodically in Johnny's father's realty business, seeing in Jeremiah Jones a kindred spirit, and this in spite of the senator's segregationist leanings. Jeremiah was not one to refuse money: where'er it came from be damned. The senator set him up with certain men in the state capitol building and in our Upcountry county and elsewhere over the state, and those connections eventually allowed the man to take over the place. By the dawn of the 1960s Jeremiah Jones had more money than anyone in three counties. But Storm expected something in return. Johnny was up late one night with me and little Sam Talbert, and Johnny's mother, Constance, had received the senator in the front room of their big house on Black Street, adjacent Main. They drank iced tea and waited, presumably, for Jeremiah.

Johnny had cigarettes, which I wanted. I climbed through his small first-floor window like this every few nights, way too late for a 12-year-old to be out. We hung there in his room in that massive house, puffing and coughing away, ever careful to blow the clouds clear of the breeze that sucked cool night air into the place.

Johnny did not tell me the senator was there, not at first. By the time he did I was lightheaded and not giggling or happy or even really thinking at all. The whole time we smoked and punched on each other, Sam, the younger brother of my buddy Tope, sat on Johnny's bed on the other side of the room with his face done up in a scowl. Johnny was acting out, surely, giving 8-year-old Sam all types of hell for his age, and at a certain point he tossed a butt out the window and turned and wobbled in mock-drunkenness across the room and laid a hard slap on little Sam's face. But the Talberts were always a tough lot. Sam didn't budge for a moment, and this made Johnny mad. "Get on out of here," he told Sam, the little Talbert, who only hung around because he wanted to be like his brother and exist in our elder company, plus he knew the senator would be here and Tope had him pumped up on the man's notoriety. Tope was a partisan to the old man's game, Storm a decorated veteran, former governor, state court judge and North Augusta district attorney, presidential candidate on the short-lived Dixiecrat ticket. Sam sprung up from the bed, spitting onto the carpet in Johnny's room, and made to exit via the door to the rest of the house. Before he got it half open, though, Johnny caught him. "You can't go in there," he said.

Sam protested but Johnny shoved him toward the open window. "Git!" he snapped, so Sam did. It was too late for him to be out, too.

"You ain't gotta be so mean to him," I said once the boy was gone, but Johnny wasn't listening, having resumed his spot on the windowsill and now with a fresh smoke between his lips. We smoked long and hard and pretty soon got thirsty. Here Johnny spent ludicrous effort clearing the air, effort that involved a big window fan aimed into the outer night and a pump bottle of Constance's perfume. We heard laughter from the interior of the house. Five minutes later he deemed the air clear, so he exited through the door headed for the kitchen to sneak a couple Cokes and on which route he heard, I know now, the unmistakable creaking of his parents' bed. He peered into the living room, and the senator Thorpe Storm and his mother were nowhere to be found. Johnny stopped on the way back to his room and heard again the unmistakable and regular thrum of bedsprings behind the closed door to his parents' bedroom and now a breathing and low moaning added to the symphony. When his father arrived an hour later, Constance and Storm were back in the living room waiting for him, but it didn't take much for young Johnny to deduce the truth of what went on that night. He told his father what he'd heard and didn't get much reaction at first, maybe a shrug from Jeremiah, a long-away look in his eyes. Years later, though, the senator would get his due.

CLOSE TO A DECADE EARLIER, BENNY JAMES DROPPED out of school and went to work for Jeremiah; me and Johnny had, at best, ten years of living between the two of us. The town's college brought around students by the truckloads. They rented from Jones, who'd tell you he fixed up the old black section of town just this side of the college all by himself, old Cherry Hill perhaps a half-mile square and full of crumbling houses by 1955, stuck between the college on one side, bleachery on the other. But Benny James seduced Jeremiah one scorching Saturday on Main Street in front of the white man's realty office. Benny hung back in the morning sun against one of the lampposts that lined the road. Jeremiah, he knew, would be in early doing his numbers. The black man Benny, cut like a bodybuilder, waited a long enough time in which to settle his nerves, and only after he knocked an opera on the little storefront door did Jeremiah finally deign to appear. Benny backed into the street as the big man poured full into the sun, head scanning up and down the sidewalk. "What do you want?" Jeremiah said, sweating through the cloth of his oxford, seeing likely just a boy in Benny James, as he would. And Benny didn't respond, didn't move even but to level a violent stare at Jones. The two men walled in front of each other for half a minute or more before Benny bothered to let on that he was looking for work this summer Saturday.

Neither blinked; cars passing by in the street slowed to gawk at the spectacle.

"I can build a house with my bare hands," Jeremiah said. "What do I need you for?"

"I, sir, can tear that down," Benny said, "rebuild it in half the time. My uncles taught me."

"I can have you lynched."

"I can cut your throat."

Benny's upper lip curled down just a little under the bottom so the top angle of his botched harelip led Jeremiah's gaze straight into his squinted eyes, high cheekbones leading down to a point with a calculated anger that could persuade anybody with lesser will. But Jeremiah had a good one himself: his lips pursed, chin dropped a little, forehead leaning into the unfortunate receiver and eyebrows raising slightly to bare the penetrating brown of his eyes.

In the heat, these two men ended their stand with a deal, a partnership formed out of mutual respect for a hardass.

Through middle and high school, from the mid-60s on, Johnny and I worked on crews headed by Benny James. He told us about his past, about the Woolworth sit-in when he'd manned the whites-only lunch counter on Main with a bunch of college blacks from Greensboro, all of whom were arrested. Benny told us how he got out of it, let straight out of his cell with the help of Johnny's father himself, who by that time pulled considerable weight in the town and county beyond.

Benny James was behind a tree watching, enraged, when a pack of men didn't pull their punches on a few of the Freedom Riders at our town's bus station in 1961. But Benny's most formidable adversary was the senator Thorpe Storm. He discussed his hatred of the man freely with us, if he didn't bring it up around Jeremiah. Storm was all white-devil magnanimity to Benny James, the senator a smiling thug of the paternally racist variety, the likes of which our state has seen over and over again and will continue to see as long as its people can remember their woeful history. "Just listen to the man," Benny would say. "He's back and forth on everything. Shit, the cracker's joined the party of Lincoln. What does that make him? The first Dixie cracker to be a member of every goddamned party available." And Benny would be right, for Storm had become a Nixon man in that year of years for party politics, 1968, when the outraged morality of those Bible jackasses began its slow turn toward siding with the eventual party of corporate economic and military might. More importantly for us that year, Storm had been named "South Carolinian of the Year" by some assuredly backward state apparatus. Accordingly the man hit the trail, honoring himself. He put in an appearance in every town in the state, Up- and Lowcountry, shaking hands and kissing babies. Mid-May hit our little hill town, and the senator was scheduled to appear in the annual spring festival parade coming straight down Main on the first float out of the gate. Benny James and Johnny had begun to revel in their mutual hatred of the man, Benny divulging a rumor he said was spread far throughout the town and of which Johnny had no knowledge: 'twas that Storm was actually Johnny's father, the old fling between Constance and Storm having been elevated in the town's mind via the classic distortion of hearsay and moved backward in time approximately twelve years, nine months prior to Johnny's birth, though you'd know it was false if you'd been smoking cigarettes in the boy's room that lonely night, or even if you knew the smallest fact about the senator and Constance. Storm's eyes shone the bright blue of the white gentry, like Constance's. Johnny's own were a murky, lake-water brown, just like Jeremiah's. Two blues won't make a brown, but logic be damned: the young man Johnny determined he'd prove the falsity to the world in ways counter to pointing out the laws of trait inheritance, or so he'd said, and I was pulled along by the force of his adamant nature, a persuasion inherent in his insanity quite impossible for my naïve mind to resist.

Johnny conspired with Benny James to fuck the parade as a last shot to the senator. It was a splendid day, sun high and bright, the whole town crowded against the canvas of a damn-near-whimsical excuse for a police barrier at the upper end of Main. We waited out the senator's float, a big white whale built up over an old police car or a jeep. Scattered among the crowd, popcorn vendors wearing red-and-white-striped uniforms wheeled their carts and accordion players danced, pumping their instruments. Mimes entranced kids. I stood in the middle of it all with my girlfriend and future wife, Liz, who hadn't a clue. I passed her a cigarette to keep her occupied. We waited for Thorpe.

Johnny threw on a Groucho glasses-and-mustache getup, parked his '64 GTO down Main Street in an alley. Benny climbed the fire escape ladder at the rear of the Woolworth's. He took a rope along with him to hoist Johnny up the back after the kid would squeeze from the passenger-side door of his wrecked car. I stayed street-level, crowd control in case the onlookers didn't go completely nuts. I'd be there to nudge them along.

Nothing but the mass out this day, the crowd roaring restless, sound consuming the street and buildings, the very air. The scene seemed to shimmer, lose its focus in the noise. I took Liz's cigarette and pulled hard on it, rubbed at my eyes with my free hand to clear the sight. The senator's float wheeled full from Spruce Street. Thorpe sat atop a big white chair, a throne reflecting the blinding sunlight. Women in summer skirts broke violently through the pathetic canvas barrier. They avoided one of the uniformed cops along the way, wailing in ecstasy for Thorpe Storm and making like they'd board the float if the platform were not so high. A number of plainclothes henchmen emerged with their guns from the mass up the street and hustled the breakers back over onto the sidewalks. I pursed my lips, worried at the show of force.

"Here he comes!" Liz pressing into my side, screaming at my ear. Men and women on both sides of the street squeezed into the scant sidewalk space, arms shot high and waving miniature flags both Union and old Dixie. Thorpe stood high midstreet, waving his own hands this way and that. A blast of a cheer launched from the revelers this side of the road, where Thorpe's eyes and spindly body now turned. "You know, Thorpe's getting old," Liz said. The sun left shadows in the wrinkles on his forehead and along his jaw, where jowls were even then beginning to form. "He looks like a damned nutcracker," Liz went on. "Like somebody's pulling the lever in back of him." Standing atop the white whale mimicking it with his pressed white suit, Thorpe retained the gall to flout the no-white-pants-prior-to-Memorial-Day adage, take it all. He waved his right hand high, now letting fly a yell of his own. He came on.

A chant rose from the horde up the street: "Thorpe '68! Thorpe '68!" the people screamed, even Liz for a moment. You'd think they could have come up with something better than that, though they whipped it good and loud like their senator was on the presidential ticket again, the old Dixiecrat. He was no Dick Nixon, though to have seen him there, that smile on his face, hands high, palms forward as if in supplication to the Almighty, quivering there in air… "Now he looks like a preacher," Liz said, nodding frantically.

And out from under the roar of the horde rose a piercing, gasoline scream. Johnny's GTO gunned from the alleyway into the street, wheeling wide and fishtailing a little before straightening and hitching as tread caught to pavement, the vehicle's body floating up on its front springs with the throttle, charting a direct course for the white whale. The crowd deflated. A collective gasp issued over even the screaming GTO, which rocketed through first, second, into third gear. "Hey-ey Johnny!" I whooped, forgetting myself for the moment. One of the accordion players went on like nothing had happened: "Hound Dog," polka-style. The mass leaned forward, keeping to the curbs as of yet, held back by the curbs, every body stretching over the shoulders of the next to see, if only to see—if only I could firmly place this in your memory. It's stuck in mine for years, sounded with the force of an explosion upon recollection. Thorpe appeared for a moment not to have even noticed the car, his arms still poised high overhead, body gleaming in that suit, in the full sun. He turned then my way, even, where I still yelled, "Go-oh Johnny! Go!" in the very glory of that moment. Thorpe's eyes went wide as finally he registered the car; his arms fell to his sides, then palms-out in front of him like he'd be able to stop it. Men in black suits emerged from the belly of the whale onto the platform. The crowd collapsed into itself, pulled in as the space between car and float vanished. BLAM!

Johnny's GTO slammed into the whale at upwards of 40 mile an hour and wrung forth yet another collective gasp. Thorpe teetered, fell to his knees, then back with his elbows on the seat of his white throne. There was a moment of near silence, here, enough time for me to register the fact that all could go horribly wrong if we didn't get to Johnny before the blacksuits. There was no movement as of yet inside of the car. The radiator began its busted steam-hiss. And with that, a second or two of reverie, the crowd wonderfully exploded. I lost sight of the car in the melee. The blacksuits on the platform jumped up quick, brandishing pistols. "That's Johnny?" Liz said. Her eyes shot wide with fear for the boy, but I only screamed, howled away in mock-agony with the crowd, men and women alike now voicing their outrage in great wails, though some laughed at each other, delighted at the calamity, flexing their destructive urges and climbing atop the GTO to kick at the roof with the heels of their Sunday shoes. I prayed that the boy was out of there. Steam continued to rise in a billowing cloud from the busted radiator. The smoke provided cover, I figured, though I must have looked senseless, guilty, wailing like a sick woman, pulling Liz around the back of the car and her asking me all the while, "What the hell are you doing, Al? Jesus! Is that Johnny's car?" I blew a steady stream of nonsense, told her to hush up in the middle of it. Then I let her go. On the far side of the car folks peered into its windows, fanned the open passenger-side door in disbelief, fanned their faces against the cloud of steam that continued to rise, through it all. I took one last look back at Liz, whose mouth opened and let fly "Albert Ledbetter Goddamnit!" before I took off running.

When I hit the roof of the Woolworth's, Johnny was already there with Benny. We argued about what to do. Benny just wanted to get out, as went our plan. Johnny seemed hell-bent on staying, and I was with Ben, truthfully. Storm was back on his feet down below, lining up the entire town against the storefronts this side of the street, handcuffs clasped down on as many folks as his blacksuits could accommodate just so he himself could then let them go. "Thorpe's really having his on this one," I offered to Johnny, who just laughed, stood up and yelled something completely unintelligible into the sky. And Storm responded, "Hey, up there! Anybody up there?" Benny and I hit the roof's tarpaper. Johnny remained standing, laughing. Down below: silence, then "Check that roof, boys!" Storm hollered. Benny absolutely refused to stay. "Meet at Henny's," he said, and took off running. When he reached the edge of the Woolworth's roof, he sprung into the air, hung there for an ever-so-brief moment before disappearing onto the lower roof of the theater. I ran and sailed right behind. In midair, things seem so small and unbelievably stupid. I turned my head on the way down, caught Johnny's silhouette caught, in turn, in the sun at the roof's edge. I landed hard on the tarpaper, going down on my hands and knees and turning back toward that black column of Johnny. He seemed to nod my way, turning then to look back over his shoulder to the street below. "Are you coming?" I asked his shape. He nodded but only stood there stupidly, like he was scared of the fall. Then he turned and walked back the other way, disappearing little by little.

BENNY AND I GOT AWAY, AND JOHNNY WAS CAUGHT; but guilt had a hard time sticking to the boy in those days. As time rolled on I wouldn't see him so much: high school graduation (a blur of caps and gowns and alcohol), hash slung fiercely my nights at the waffle shop by the interstate, where he'd occasionally stop on his way elsewhere after the highway was laid down at the edge of town. I moved to a trailer in Commerce, Georgia, then, while Johnny was in college in Athens; I saw him there. My father, who left me and my whacked mother when I was 12, taught biology science and literature in Athens. Johnny never had him for a class, I don't think, nor thankfully did I have to sit and listen to whatever holy lie he filled his students with. Though there, in Commerce, my proximity to him afforded me all sorts of favors care of his teacher's salary. I somehow managed to wreck five cars in two years, junkers he bought me like to pay me off. He was responsible, likewise, for the silver trailer I lived in. I set it up just off the newly laid I-85, got a job slinging hash at another waffle shop, and a tornado came through and dropped a mammoth oak tree right on top of my trailer, buckling the roof and requiring a climb through the window to exit, if happen you were stuck inside, which I was. Such has been my luck.

I got back to Carolina. I worked at the bleachery for 20 years until four or so ago when the checks from Johnny started coming in. He paid me monthly for visits to his son Bobby Jones, named after the famous golfer, in the county penitentiary. I went down there every week. He's been locked away going on ten years for the killing of his mother, Johnny's wife Betty, an act that killed my wife as well: she died of a heart attack shortly after she heard the news.

I deliver Bobby his prison whiskey, which he likes. The guards know Johnny, knew Jeremiah even better when he was alive, so they let me. I take him letters Johnny sends, which the boy refuses to read. Letters from his older brother Billy he'll glance at, though he cries his way through them. I withhold judgment. The pay is good.

I sit on the porch of this rented house.

Johnny is a rich man. When Jeremiah died a decade back, my sometime friend threw an outrageous party at the lake. I had not seen the man since that party, nor heard from him but for the checks, his signature arriving at my porch monthly to shock me dumb. And then he walked up from the street wearing a black cowboy hat and boots, still with his hair down to his shoulders but now streaked here and there with gray. He hung around in the yard for a moment. I didn't recognize him at first. When finally I did, I told him he looked like he'd joined a damned rodeo. Chaps, even, covered his ratty jeans. "My horse is tied up to that big oak in your backyard," he mock-drawled, then added, "rode it up from Anderson," like it wasn't anything for him to do. Anderson was three hours away in a car.

I was surprised to see him, horse or not, but the shock of it didn't propel me from the porch, out of my chair. Though I did take my feet from the front railing, sit up a little, reach out and grab the full ashtray from the railing and dump it into the bushes. I set the ashtray back, did not even speak. I watched and waited, outraged, for the man to come up and say a few words, like I figured he needed to if he was to explain what would compel a man to ride a horse 200 miles to arrive unannounced at my dumpy porch.

He did, eventually, and talked.

Seems Johnny Jones the lost soul had realized a dream; he fashioned a ranch out of two square miles of property between Anderson and Greenville on which a crumbling old house sat. I told him his son was getting on in prison, a strange kid, but he always was a quiet sort. "What the hell happened to Benny James?" I asked after a time, genuinely curious, and Johnny's eyes lit up at the question. But he did not answer. He lingered on his father instead, and we got around as always to the day of the parade, Johnny's act of vengeance spawned, also, by his father.

"Mayor Ridley was there that day," he said. "Gerald Stowe too. When I finally got out of the car, did you know I saw Ridley come out of the old drug store crying his eyes out? Stowe was laughing at him, even." Gerald Stowe was the foggy mind behind the bumbling windbag of Ridley, the one-term mayor. Jeremiah had run the town, essentially. That's how you could put it. He had the most money.

I began pouring whiskey for the two of us, and we got on a healthy drunk. Sitting there listening to him talk on, I became aware of the pattern of it all, the years, the very fact that I knew he'd seen Ridley all teary-eyed and Stowe laughing at the man; I'd heard him tell me this story sundry occasions. A day or two after the parade, for instance, down at the Manetta mill pond with a couple no-good moonshiners the boy knew and who were given to indulging his fancy. That and getting him drunk. *And and and Ridley wipes his tears with a sleeve of that heinous blue serge jacket he wears. Stowe looks like he wants to howl in laughter, see, cause his boss is taking the degradation personally, taking it like it's his own fault, and well if you were to look at the man's record you'd know it's true. Like my Daddy says, the only way to get on is treat them like they ain't human at all, if you want something from them. And the goddamned senator is making a laughingstock out of everyone. He clearly has no use for Ridley, who stands the whole time back against the glass front of the drug store with Stowe watching Thorpe Storm go down the line of our teachers and friends and neighbors unclasping their handcuffs just so he can get his paw in, so he can reassure them that they are not in any way under suspicion for the act. My wrecked car, all the while, blows up steam from the radiator, and the other standing floats cascade from the wreck back up past the Baptist church and around the corner at the Episcopalian, a damned beautiful sight, yes, and I'm laughing up on the roof by now, laughing away Albert, ain't that right? And Daddy comes striding up from the low end of the street and Ridley and Stowe take notice, my Daddy in his own blue suit and striding up like a billiards shark with the absolute foreknowledge of victory. He ain't got a doubt, you see. Ridley comes out through the line of handcuffed to meet him. That line, meant to be broken, of course, and God bless fatass Ridley for doing it. Ridley waddles between a mother and her sorry handcuffed son, paying no attention, and the both of them slit their eyes when he passes like they can't believe the sleight. Goddamn sweet freedom for all! But Daddy catches Ridley then in a stare in the middle of the street. Stowe looks like he'd die of laughter. He's trying hard to hold it back, but he can't. Ridley there and that outrageous paunch of his gut and a fly then landing square on his nose. My Daddy stares on and stares on and on, for he can see two feet in front of him, and Ridley ain't got a chance, nor Storm. Daddy's got it fixed, you can be sure. And Stowe probably knows this, and does something only to justify the gut-busting laughter he's got coming on. He looks over to fat Clyde the police chief, who all this time's been down on his haunches over by the car and float and here and there pulling his walkie-talkie to squawk calls for fire vehicles and such. Stowe gets Clyde going on about the nigger joke where the guy driving a Cadillac's an unapologetic racist and hits blacks with his car and notches the dashboard for each one he's laid off. Clyde starts in on it to Stowe and Stowe's stomach caves in with the laughter. He wants it to be like he's laughing at the joke, not at his boss who's getting the stare-down from Daddy, standing there like a fantastic sportsman, Daddy, a hard man, but you've gotta respect him. Clyde's in on the guilty terminology, of course, using the language quite liberally, and he gets Thorpe Storm's notice. One of Storm's blacksuits is having a damned time trying to keep a straight face at the joke himself. Cause everybody in both Carolinas knows the punch line, and if that's your kind of thing, so be it, but Clyde's getting to the part where the Cadillac driver's picked up his Reverend, who's out of gas and of course making the driver feel guilty as hell cause the Caddy man, before he picked up the Reverend, thought the Reverend was a black man and he was veering over to hit him when he realized his mistake. As chief Clyde says, "Yeah, 'well if it ain't,' the Reverend says, and then, 'We ain't seen you in church in quite some time.' And the Caddy man apologizes to the Reverend for missing the service-after-service, surely, and offers him a ride to the gas station. The Revered jumps in with the empty gas can and gives the Caddy man a soft little chiding. And the Caddy man is feeling awful, just awful, and it ain't too long before coming up the road what do we see but—" and Storm's blacksuit belts out "A nigger!" and Stowe howls laughter and Ridley quivers under Daddy's gaze, still, and Thorpe Storm stops his handshaking and wheels around, pipes up in that imperious whine of his, "Son! We do not use that word, now, do we?" The blacksuit got straight quick, "A—a black man," he said, under Storm's fiery eyes, which now finally took notice of Daddy there with Ridley like a scared deer in the headlights of his eyes, and Storm tells my Daddy very gracefully to leave the poor mayor be, he ain't worth the time. But Daddy plays it hard, doesn't look away atall from Ridley, then accuses Ridley of blaming me, his very son, for this wreck here, saying that Jeremiah Jones the fantastic sportsman will not be having any of these false accusations flying. But Ridley ain't even said anything, and it's clear that everybody knows I did it, including Storm, who also knows why, when he was for so long putting that withered old pecker of his in my mother, and then he says "Well your son like to have killed me!" Clyde's whispering to the blacksuit, now, and I imagine it like: "You're right, son, a nigger," and Stowe's howling away, leaning in close with Clyde and the blacksuit but keeping an eye on the goings-on at his side, as his boss Ridley is being destroyed here in that stare and Daddy is getting accosted by the senator, whose brow furrows violently, his ass hitching up like somebody just stuck a cob up in it, and Stowe can't do nothing but laugh. Clyde whispers on, "And the Caddy man, it's all he can do to keep listening to the Reverend going on and on and on about this and that, about so-and-so's mother who's in the hospital or, well, the kind of shit Reverends go on about. The Caddy man has set his sights on the nigger up ahead, and it's all he can do to keep from hitting the poor guy." And the cob in Thorpe Storm's asshole is covered in some kind of bayou hot sauce and being wedged in, wrung from side to side and top to bottom. Because Daddy, Stowe seeing it all, out of hard vengeance won't even hardly acknowledge Storm. Clyde goes, "Well, the Caddy man at the last second pulls the car back from the side of the road just before hitting the black man. But there's this thud like he did."*

"Look here, Jeremiah!" Thorpe Storm pipes in.

"The Caddy man, he looks to the Reverend, and he says, 'Now, Reverend,' he says, 'did I hit that man walking back there?'"

Storm saying "Look here! Jeremiah, for God's sake, look here!"

"—and the Reverend looks to the Caddy man. He says, 'The nigger? No way, you missed, but it's okay—'"

"Jeremiah, son!"

"'—cause I got him with the gas can!'" Clyde bellowed the punch line; I heard that one all the way up top, about the time Albert and Benny James fled the roof, and the senator's blacksuits come up behind me to cuff me and take me away, but not before Storm turns to Clyde and Stowe and his blacksuit, speaking his piece to Clyde, saying, "I've heard that one, big man," Clyde of course with his outrageous gut bigger than Ridley's and my Daddy's combined. "Not funny," Thorpe says, and Stowe ain't laughing no more. "Get up son," says Thorpe Storm to his howling blacksuit, and Clyde says, "To each his own," cause he don't give a goddamn. I could hear them

behind me now, coming up from the fire escape on to the back edge of the roof, and Storm threw his body between Daddy and Mayor Ridley, who fell hard to the ground, sweating and dirtying up the blue serge coat. "Je – re – mi – ah," Storm said, now in diplomatic mode, his hand going to Daddy's shoulder. "Now what do you have against the mayor here? He's clearly not worth the time." You can hear him, all six foot of slimy politician.

Daddy repeats that Ridley has insulted his son, and he will not have it.

The boys then called out from the roof of the Woolworth's. They had me. "Johnny!" Daddy says. "Yessir!" I shot back.

"Come on down!" And so I did.

WHENEVER HE TELLS IT I CAN SEE IT MYSELF AND finish it for him, as he tends to switch his viewpoint down to that of the crowd. Johnny the consummate showman, forever able to suss out his audience's need, whether said audience be a couple moonshining waste-aways or myself, here on my porch now going on drunk, and Johnny having approached something like glee in the telling, himself forever amazed at the very fact of his memory of it. We might even have ended it in unison: "And they pulled the young rapscallion away from the roof's edge, his body disappearing little by little."

"Goddamnit," I said. "But you can't have seen all that you claim, and that disgusting joke!"

He pushed his cowboy hat up above the crown of his head. "You always say that," he said. "But I did. And we were wrong that day, Al. Wrong to do what we did." But he wouldn't take it back for a second, I know, just because he's old and I'm old and it don't take much over 30 before you realize the fallibility inherent in all your schemes. He kept talking. I kept the whiskey flowing, and night descended dark and hot around us.

Johnny was caught that day, yes, but Jeremiah was in the street putting the fear of God into Ridley and Storm both. But in that moment up there on the roof I was not sure Johnny wanted this. I thought he would go down for it to spite Storm. Me and Benny, at Henny's, the black cafe then in the last remaining quadrant of the old Cherry Hill, could see no credence atall in what Johnny'd professed about his reasoning, nor our own. An attempt on the life of a politician was a hell of a thing to pull just because your mama had a sex life too. What I do know is that Jeremiah would run for mayor some time after this and win, with the support of none other than Thorpe Storm himself. There's ways to sway a man, I say, ways like having your son run his car into the man's float.

THE ONLY OTHER 1964 GTO IN TOWN WAS A BLACK man's. Willis, manservant to Mr. and Mrs. Eugene Craig, an unlikely pair of schoolteachers and stock-market swindlers who kept Willis in an improvised room under the porch of their house on Route 5. He had one near identical to Johnny's. Willis ended up taking the hit. Benny told me a few years on that he figured Willis had been paid to do it, last minute, and the money had likely gone to the manservant's family down in Columbia. So it was a charity case, generally, and Willis came out the goddamned saint of it all, because he'd spend years in jail for the act.

Johnny claimed beforehand he hadn't told his father, but Jeremiah knew. So we can think, and think and infer, and extrapolate and say that Jeremiah Jones arrived at the scene of the wreck and had the manservant Willis's GTO airlifted to the backyard of his home so as to look like it'd been sitting there all along. More likely Jeremiah stole the thing outright, or had somebody steal it. Folks later told me it was sitting deep green in the sun and Johnny's license plate was hung to the back of it. And Benny James was there, folks told, among the crowd, having left me after 30 minutes at the cafe. Believable, I guess, though if I never got corroboration from Johnny I never would have accepted any of it. And my friend Tope told me near ten years later that he himself was at the Jones house off Black Street and saw Benny James shaking hands with Senator Thorpe Storm, on the damned garage roof, even. Power corrupts absolutely, or something. If I was a reverend and had the ear of God I guess I might go around killing people too.

The night rode on. At a certain point, Johnny stood up from his chair and shouted into the street, spilling his whiskey on the way and making a damned clattering mess of it just by my feet. I got up, figuring I'd bring the bottle out, when Willis walked up, hair all kinked up in a big ratty afro. He didn't say a word, just walked up with his hand out for some change. I gasped at the sight. "Get away from here," Johnny spat, but I was reaching in my pocket. Willis could see as much and didn't move. His eyes caught mine. "Go on. Git," Johnny said.

I tossed a quarter his way, then felt horrible because it missed his hand and Willis had to root around in the dirt to find it. But he did find it, finally, stood tall as his stooped posture would let him, and shuffled on down the road toward the center of town. Johnny sat, placing his boots firmly on the rail to watch Willis go, Johnny muttering to himself things about propriety, about men making their own way. I didn't bother to point out the grand contradictions, the fact that a little self-effacement might go a long way toward helping him get through this night without causing a fight, without alienating the only man who might give him the time of day to sit and talk it all out. "Do you even know who that was?" I asked him, and he did not. I didn't press him, but I did get mad. "And what about Benny James?" I said. Last I heard, years ago, he was a sort of lawman over in Greenville. "I mean I've asked you about the man four times in the past two hours—" Johnny pulled his boots violently from the rail, sending my ashtray clattering into the yard. He rocked forward and now stood full above me. "Albert, that's why I came," he said.

"What? To break my damned ashtray? My fucking porch rail?"

"Benny's gone," he said. I guess I had been expecting as much. It made a little sense, didn't it? Didn't much matter, I guess. So Benny James was dead. But we went on and talked and talked about the old man. He was something we could hang onto as the evening progressed into drunken obeisance to history.

"You know how he got that sheriff job, don't you?" Johnny said.

"What do you mean how he got it? You gotta run for that sort of thing."

"Well, he ran," Johnny said, "but we rigged it."

"We?"

"Yeah, me and Daddy, before he died."

"But Jeremiah hated Benny James," I said, which was the apparent truth. The two had a falling out just as hardassed as their falling in, a thing surrounding the parade, even, Jeremiah never approving of James's involvement in the act, though 'twas his own mind that concocted it.

"Daddy hated him, sure," Johnny said, "but it was more of a kind of hate-cause-he-could-hate-and-had-once-been-annoyed-by-the-man's-equality thing. At bottom he loved Ben. Then I guess he felt bad about firing him cause Ben ended up in some kind of factory when he moved to Greenville. Can you believe that goddamned Thorpe Storm's still in office?" Johnny had a way with people, he did, and this last proclamation, question, whatever it was, had the effect of wiping the reddened side of my mind clean; I laughed loud and long, tears spilling from my eyes, head falling forward and just missing the edge of the porch rail.

"What is he—300 years old by now?" I said.

"More like a thousand," Johnny said.

Benny James is dead and that damned Thorpe Storm is still running right along grabassing with Senate pages and interns, calling people niggers on camera, making a complete mockery of his home state. Benny James is dead. It doesn't mean much to me, in the end. I'm not sorry about it. I mean, it doesn't really make me sad. I'm wondering mostly if that's news important enough to compel a man to ride a horse 200 miles to tell it.

JOHNNY TRIED TO GET ME OUT TO SOME BAR OR other all night. He wanted to go to the Long Branch, a country-western club out by the interstate. I told him it figured he'd want to go there, with a grand sweep of a gesture to indicate the black cowboy hat, his chaps. "No point in leaving, though, this late," I said. I settled back in my chair and watched him from the corner of my eye. When he didn't speak, I began to tell him how Tope won a year's supply of whiskey in a raffle put on by an upstart distillery in North Carolina.

"Those boys took on more than they bargained for," he laughed. Tope was a mighty man, 300 pounds or more, who could take down a fifth all at once and may not even show the telltale signs of it. I poured a couple more for ourselves and we talked on into the darkness. He told me about his son Billy, who I knew was living away his time in the Disneyfied world of Chicagoland. I raised my glass, he raised his, and we downed them. I got up to make us another, but Johnny rose too, now. "The boy is a traitor to his upbringing," Johnny said. The single bulb on my porch blew a fierce light into those eyes of his, the cowboy hat still pushed back atop his head. "He is wrong, too." Johnny is a moral man, a soul set in high gear. "Maybe you're wrong now," I said. I could say that much—could think it, too, that if mistakes were being made here, they were his own. I wobbled indoors to put a lid on that sort of talk, but he wouldn't have it. He followed me in, scribbled a number on the yellow pad by my telephone and told me to call Billy, tell him his father was coming to see him. "I know now," he went on. "My own father's money. I'm using it and not making a dime off it. Do you know that? I'll use it till it's spent and I have to go out and get a job washing dishes, or maybe as senile Storm's aide, anything. I've set up a goddamned ranch in Carolina. I'm paying the hands. We're gone drive them!" he said.

"You're drunk," I said, pouring a couple more. "My God! That's distasteful talk."

"You tell Billy I'm coming for him, at least," he said, and pulled from a pocket four $100 bills. "A complete and total aberration!" Johnny was agitated. I handed him the whiskey and made to move around him back to the porch when he stopped me with a hand to my chest. "I love it! I pay them and I pay you and I love it!" The man is at least a tad crazy, I think. He pays me because he's too chickenshit to face the fruit of his loins, which took his own sweet wife from him, one among a trail of dead fallen along behind him, leading back to whatever asshole fell off the boat that brought his people here. And he was trying to send me a thousand miles north to the other, who I knew couldn't bear the blood, who knew too well where any sort of moral fault lay. The depthless eyes of the shambling drunk Willis sprung into my mind magnified by electric light, the electric light that shown in Johnny's own, the gleam staring up above my head into its own self-immolating dream. His would be his own undoing, as my professor father Hank Ledbetter must have quoted to me from some textbook or other. The pattern was clear, and despite all I missed my friend even as he stood square in front of me.

He nearly did give up, though, came real close to settling in for an easy, slow night, but I was apparently not long for this world. I don't recall how it ended, and when I woke in the morning the rain poured down on my shoes. Johnny was gone. I raised my head from the back of the rocking chair, took my soaked feet from the porch rail. I stood up, noted our two empty glasses, the $400 in my wallet, then went to the backyard and got down on my hands and knees in the mud around the old oak, flinging wet grass and dirt and bits of bark looking hopelessly for hoof prints, just to confirm. I never did get a look at that horse he was talking about.

And that made me sad, if only for a minute. In the end, all's well. I'm still here. I like my porch. I like my whiskey. I like that damned classic sports network—based up the road in Charlotte, they package it with even the most low-grade cable deal—whenever I muster up the will to get off the porch long enough to watch. It's raining today, and that's fine. Maybe I will make it to Chicago, though Johnny will have to spread the love, the money, further. I've got Billy's phone number, anyway, on the little pad by the phone.

Billy

ALBERT'S ADVICE TO ME THAT UNSEASONABLY COLD Independence Day was decidedly less pristine than A.H.'s old dictum. "So you mean to tell me you've got a perfectly good girl who's mad at you cause you puked your guts out in your own drawer, and you're hung up on a goddamned lesbian? My God, boy, buy the puke-drawer some flowers or something and get over it. That or you might as well shoot yourself in the head. You still got that pistol. Or did I hear you say you gave it back?"

Albert could be counted on for laughs, if all else failed. He suggested that I take a long walk, then hit a bar and get hammered. That always helped him, he said. "You'll wake up tomorrow a new man. Won't remember a thing for a few days, at least. And when you do remember, go out and do it all over again." So I did, once I got off the phone.

I wore my Confederate gray topcoat with the golden buttons fastened all the way to my throat. It was cold for July, anyway: by nightfall Chicago had dropped into the 50s, and I felt a little surly in the face of my plan, absurdly prideful of the great heehawing state of South Carolina. I didn't get to wear the coat enough these days. It was a beautiful thing, and its history, the known half of it anyway, was a miracle to behold.

When I was 17 my brother Bobby's geek friend Jared had a wild story that he passed Bobby's way one day on the middle-school basketball court. Bobby brought the news to me, and I told him first off that it was likely a load of shit. But my father told stories about that mill pond on Fishing Creek, the rope swing he and his friends, back in the 1950s, had quite a time on: for instance one friend, Andy—"Stump," they called him, 5'5" but built like a tank and with arms akin to those of a certain cartoon sailor—was forever fearful of the rope, scared half to death of making a swing, preferring simply to sit on the bank and watch. Stump, one fateful day, was just drunk enough, or the other boys' cruelty was sufficiently grating to induce a quake in his bones, some feeling of required action, that he did take an inaugural swing, backing up the creek's bank, rope in hand, steely-eyed against the profound and awed silence of his compatriots. He ran, jumping and careening out over the muddy water, holding tightly to the rope, eyes wide, and then only to reach the hanging precipice of the arcing swing still holding on, not a thought in his mind of letting go and spoiling down into the water. He swung back and banged hard into the trunk of the leaning oak tree to which the rope swing was attached. My Pop Johnny Jones always told us that story with a pregnant pause at the moment we were supposed to imagine the impact, telling us how "the very ground did shake" when Stump Andy hit the tree, then received a hefty dose of rope burn as his grip loosened just enough for him to slide down and into the water. "We thought he'd like to have died," Pop would say. "But Stump was a tough kid, became a tough man too. Works at the bleachery last I heard."

There were many, many stories, such as the one about the time Pop and the boys swung to see whosoever could skim the upwelling of long-cooled magma that rose from the depths of Fishing Creek, out in the center of the mill pond, whosoever could drop in right next to the big rock without hitting it, and Pop, Johnny Jones, the young boy not yet my father or violent reactionary either, ran and jumped and knew, sailing out over that water, that he'd gone too far this time. He hung on until he couldn't no more, swung way out over the rock and then released, plummeting and busting up his shins when he splashed into the six inches of water on the rock's other side.

Or the night the boys built a bonfire on the bank to singe the hair on their toes as they swung through, failing to reckon the attraction the light would make to water moccasins, one and then two and four and seven of whom peeked their heads out of the water, slithering straight toward the beacon.

I'd been to the mill pond once, the rope swing amazingly intact or at least replaced by a new one 20 and some years later at the site of the abandoned Manetta textile mill. I drove a girlfriend, my first long-term girlfriend Katie Jones (no relation, of course), down for a debauched evening, only to have my little bare-butts party interrupted by a couple country hicks who came down to the pond for a swing on the rope. I was humiliated: caught with my pants down without even a bush other than Katie Jones's to hide behind. The girl told me what for. I'd wait months for another chance like that.

But after Bobby divulged his geek friend's tale, the place caught me unawares, loomed in my mind in spite of the "load of shit" proclamation I'd given the boy. I spent days thinking on it. *Ghosts! Of all things! Skeletons of dead Confederates buried within the rubble of the mill!* Though Bobby seemed to have forgotten the matter entirely by the time I decided I had to know. And Bobby, of all people, would have to be the person to accompany me. I'd tried every friend I had, but none was around. I was scared, I'll say, the junked box of the main mill and the rubble throughout, the stupid talk of ghosts. Bobby was a natural wimp, and if he couldn't provide an example of courage, at least he might have kept me distracted from my own fear. *Ghosts!* Totally preposterous, though I was of course unconvinced of my own conviction. I stormed into the house on a Friday. "Goddamnit, come on," I barked, grabbing the boy and pulling him from the couch. Bobby sniffled and whined in the seat of my Nova all the way out there.

"You said it was shit," he reminded me.

"Yes, I did," I said, but I couldn't get the possibility of the story's veracity out of my mind. Jared the geek had alleged, very specifically I might add, a skeleton in a Confederate uniform sitting upright in a chair in the mill's defunct office. He said he'd seen it firsthand with a couple country hicks who took him in there: Jared the geek's grandmother lived in a house in the old mill village of Lando that surrounded the place. My drunken father's stories, at the same time, included lore about an ancestor named Colquitt, my great-grandmother's maiden name, who was an infantryman during the Civil War and went crazy and killed himself during the period of the reconstruction after claiming he saw a Yankee doctor turn into a gigantic chicken. Said Colquitt did have a son before that, though, and said son worked in the mill as a man, as my father told it. The tenuous connections drove me forward that day, and when we got there the stories bore fruit, if they weren't entirely corroborated. I found the topcoat—likely a replica, but Confederate through and through—and a pair of woolen gray pants folded up on a dusty chair in the old office of the crumbling main mill. As I gathered them, I heard voices echoing through the cracked walls of the place. I shuddered, banged my way out and caught three young hicks trying to get into my car. Bobby sat on the hood looking like he might burst into tears at any moment, his pants pockets turned outward like wagging tongues. I yelled at the boys, two of whom turned tail and ran back toward the mill pond. The biggest of the three, though, was caught between me and the car, and he ran the other way, down the old outlet road that, I knew, dead-ended not a quarter mile down around another dilapidated building. When I caught the boy I whipped him with the heavy flashlight I carried, and I felt sorry about it later, because I didn't know him, and all he'd done really was steal the 12 cents my brother was carrying in his pockets, but in that moment I was on fire, enraged at the gall of the kid, my kin being so confronted. The reaction scared me a little, later, and forever I'd associate that coat with my redneck tendency to spring at the slightest provocation, something I normally kept checked. If I was wearing the coat, and drunk, things often turned out differently.

I threw it on in moments of utter desperation. The coat was consequently full of holes ripped by provoked strangers. I'd stitched them shut with blue and yellow yarn, very haphazardly, over the years, to the point that the moniker of "General" certain of my friends gave me had morphed into "Joseph," the descendant of Abraham who wore the Satanic "coat of many colors." If I was my friends, I might have dubbed myself the motley fool or at least something a little less religious or high-sounding. But Joseph it was, for them.

When I got out into the street that day on my quest to follow Albert's prescription for my pain, I promptly ran into Barry, the guitarist, who indeed greeted me with a quick "What's up?" followed by "Isn't it a little warm for that coat, Joseph?"

"False summer," I said. Barry was a Virginian who moved to Chicago and joined an alt-country act that got pretty big for a time early in the 90s, but whose heyday had passed. I walked on after talking briefly with him about nothing, thinking now of another Virginian, my old friend Kate, who worked in the bar at the Hotel Fermata, a swank number down in the Loop that catered to rock 'n' roll bands and business-tripping Internet-bubble executives and other beneficiaries of the fading "new economy." Kate was a "sales associate," and she played the part well between stints behind the bar. Certain days of the week the place was open to "clients," and Kate's job was to sell them on the hip climes for their future accommodation needs—a great deal of the selling was simply free booze and finger food. She sold me to her boss as a rock 'n' roll agent the first time I stopped by. I wore my leather pants and, indeed, the Confederate gray. I told the man I was from Nashville, speaking all the while in a Southern accent three degrees thicker than my normal slur, and he gave Kate full license to treat me like a king, which she did.

But I abused the privilege, went back again and again and again. And at one point her boss began to get wise to the gag. Kate told him, "He's a tough cat," selling it to the boss that I just would not make up my mind about the hotel for all my rock 'n' country clients, likely losing a few points with the man, or making it look like she was just "after" me personally, which maybe he could at least relate to. In fact, I'd always wondered why she and I hadn't hit it off in more than just our chummy way. Maybe we drank too much, or not enough. Maybe her hometown Virginia tales matched up too exactly with my SC stories, and we never had anything to build from. But anyway her boss told her not to bring me in again, so I was out, at least till I got a haircut and bought a suit, or borrowed one of A.H.'s outfits.

Quite a long time had passed, since then, and I wasn't wearing my leather pants this Independence Day, so I trod on. Kate was there, and surprised to see me. "Haven't you heard the news?" I said, my favorite greeting.

"Thorpe Storm is dead?" she said, her favorite response, already pouring me a beer from the Fermata's single tap.

"Not yet, unfortunately," I cracked, "but the flag came down from the capitol today, and the old man was happy as a bedbug. They put it on the grounds right out front. You oughta see it."

"You ain't been celebrating, I take it."

"Oh no. But the South Carolinian's Independence Day is a long way away, don't you know?" Kate looked perplexed. "March 5, 1877, inauguration day for Hayes. End of the reconstruction," I said, and Kate put the beer in front of me as we laughed. I raised the glass and tipped it her way before downing it in two or three gulps. She poured me another. It wasn't long before I was ripped, just as Albert had advised, but I hadn't forgotten anything: I began talking about Sofie and Elsa and A.H. and all of them, and Kate kept the drinks flowing strong and joined in herself, throwing back one after another of her typical Pernod and water in the empty place, this fine day, and as she closed early—it must have been nearly midnight—I sat at the bar, fighting for balance on the stool.

By some turn that I cannot and will likely never remember, I started as if coming out of a dream at my doorstep, and Kate was chattering behind me about how she couldn't believe what she was doing and giggling high and wild in between and I at least comprehended the inevitable all right there and tried the rest of the time to fully commit myself to the act. And I could not, remembering my dried-up puke in the bottom drawer of the dresser and Kate with her round face up above me, her dark hair—I could think of no one but Elsa as Kate bounced along above me, grunting strangely, and I woke the next morning unable to recall how it ended, assuming I'd passed out, and rolled cautiously off my side to my back to find the little twin bed otherwise empty.

And I felt horrible about it all, like I'd felt the first time I'd ever had sex, with the other Kate I took down to the mill pond, later on in my parents' bed of all places, sick at the transgression of it all, conflating the two in my hungover mind, maybe. But Albert was right, in the end. I forgot the rest in the weeks ahead, even after Sofie'd called to tell me she wasn't coming back and could I please put her stuff in a parcel and mail it to her? It wasn't much, after all. I did it the very day she called, a few weeks on, put it all in a box and sent it after ridding the stuff of the puke stains. And goddamn them all, I was thinking by now: my route toward happiness via women was marred with so many disasters. I didn't need an ally. I needed an enemy. I turned on the evening news one night around this time and was witness to the most serendipitous sight: the feet of U.S. Senator Thorpe Storm sticking out into the aisle of the Senate hall in the Capitol in Washington. He'd collapsed in the middle of a vote and the networks were carrying it live.

Damned to the margins of national politics though he was, being from South Carolina during any administration, he was the oldest and longest-serving U.S. senator in the nation. Storm was 99 going on 100 at this point, and though the possibility of his death was ever present in the mind of many a liberal Carolinian, it was not cause for national coverage, I thought. But this macabre spectacle, in that burgeoning age of so-called reality-TV programming, turned out too much to resist. Storm was laid out and there were his feet and there was Ted Kennedy of all people leaning over him and paramedics eventually rushing into the hall. My phone rang.

It was Albert.

"You watching this shit?" he said.

"Yep."

"Just wanted to make sure." He hung up.

My father's old nemesis—for Johnny Jones most certainly had an enemy to get him through his younger days—was passed out on the floor, and then the cameras cut to a press conference with our shit-eating president, the unelected Texan, who lamented the sadness already of Storm's death. And I thought very clearly that if anyone needed an enemy at this point in our history, here he stood: he was being fed to us daily on the television screen. I reveled in the hate that I felt at that moment, a hate undefined by any particular issue, but ever present nonetheless. If Thorpe Storm was dead, the Texan would do just fine for an enemy.

BUT STORM WASN'T DEAD. THE PRESIDENT HAD IT ALL wrong, per usual. Albert would call me back later in the day, long after I'd accepted the truth of the press conference and assumed the best for the state of South Carolina. Turns out it'd been one in a long line of strokes that left the former segregationist unable to walk without the help of his aides. The people of the state were jubilant, Albert said. "Even the goddamned newscasters are having a fine time keeping their happiness in check. It's pitiful," he spat.

Folks continued election after election to vote for the old man, I felt, for no reason other than spite offered to the rest of the nation as thanks for SC's underfunded schools, the nation's cruel punishment of it for its insurrectionist past—an idea that was drilled into the children there from an early age in direct contradiction of the truth. If anyone was responsible for all the hell the state had seen, it was SC herself. Still, we all knew the old boys of post-1865 Carolina had their enemies. Sampson Colquitt, for instance, my insane ancestor, knew or at least thought he knew who his enemy was. My father told me that story over and over and over again, nights by the fireplace in the old house on Main he'd inherited from my grandfather. He'd use it as a sort of history lesson for me and my brother: taking the point of view of the young Colquitt, he stood while he told it. I had, consequently, a false definition in my head of the word *croup* for years to come. *Ephus Kennedy rode a shiny black buggy into Yorkville. It was summer and I was sick with that infernal croup. Coughing, and coughing, it never did stop me, though. I met the fat doctor and coughed my way down to the meeting of the Yorkville Donkey Floggers With Golden Riding Sticks, so named on account of the Yankee ban. After they took the county militia, they had the gall then to ban our clubs. Damn the governor! The Yankee! as Oglethorpe says. We figure if the occupation thinks we're out here riding donkeys bareback all is well.*

Old cavalry officer Oglethorpe himself had renamed the club, actually. He had all the ideas. He could twirl a pistol piece like a Yankee dandy. And when I got down to the barren cotton field where we convened that day, like every other, Thorpe stood in his old gray uniform, leg up on an old oak stump, whipping the piece up, twirling it thrice backward, stopping it pointed down and back like a sheathed sword. He thrust his chest out there in the sunlight, now atop the stump, and spun the pistol piece back the other way, thrice again, thrusting it with an iron-black plunge into its holster. He gazed all round our ranks. We held our arms crossed for a long moment, our own shoddy weaponry, guns we had nary a whit of confidence in, holstered for the moment. But when Oglethorpe finally raised his pistol into the air and fired, we grasped our pieces with our whole hearts and hands and fired ourselves, the sound banging out into the air of the clearing.

Thorpe raised his chin when it was over. Ever since he come back from the war, he did raise it like that. He used to wear a danged powder wig from last century, his bearing regal. Now that his head was exposed cause he was broke like the rest of us, and his actual hair was so thin and wispy there at the crown above his brow, raising his chin was about all Thorpe could do to summon any dignity atall. He jumped now fully atop the stump, eyes slit to a black line as he gazed out over us. He raised a fist. "I call this meeting of the Yorkville Donkey Floggers With Golden Riding Sticks to session!" he hollered. He raised his pistol and fired into the air again. The lot of us laughed because the name sounded so danged stupid, though down in Columbia, the Flying Artillery had become the Musical Club With Four Twelve Pounder Flutes. The boys around me cheered and laughed and raised their guns. The shots blew clear skyward with their laughter, but I just coughed. Gunpowder smoke came near to choking me. I'd do anything to get rid of that croup. I coughed and coughed, doubled over, spit and dry-heaved down into the dirt of the clearing. An old jaybird came swooping down from a pine at the edge of the field and took a lock of hair right from my own scalp.

The boys kept laughing, now at my expense. My face must have been near red as Wade Hampton's boys' shirts, which might have been a good thing, but for the laughing. They kept it up, and I kept coughing.

Then, during one of my wheezing gasps for breath, the raucous laughter cut off down to a murmur and the field fell silent. I heard a crow caw way back in the big woods behind us. I barked another cough, sucked it in.

Thorpe hopped from the stump now and walked out among us. "First order of business!" he hollered, ignoring my wheezing. "That carpetbagging Ephus Kennedy has set up camp selling medicine and claiming to be healing people! Like he's some kind of god born to the great South and has the right—the right! by God!—to be ministering to our children and teaching them the voodoo ways of the slaves he set free! Will we let him?"

Thorpe received a rousing chorus of "Hell No!"s to this. I stood up and tried to join in, but only did get out a little yelp before the croup began to rally in my chest.

I flew over at the force of this one, hit the dirt with a thump and damned painful wheeze. The boys ignored me in their fervor. Thorpe went on, "We have got to hit this Yankee where he lives, do you hear me? He's big and as unhealthy as any of the boys and girls he treats, much less whatever hellhole he comes from. Even sicker than you, Sampson." I raised my head slowly from the dust. My chest heaved, burned, but I sucked the feeling down and gazed up at Thorpe, who'd lowered his chin a bit for me. I smiled a little, then burst into another barking fit for the effort, blowing up a brown cloud of dust from the ground in front of me. Laughter roared back up from the boys. "Yes," Thorpe chuckled, "Sampson here's even been to see the fat Yankee doctor, which we of the great South are committed—yes!—committed to driving from our township! Now have you not, Sampson? And are you any better?"

I could summon nary a muscle, splayed heaving down in the dirt as the boys laughed on. And yes, I had been to see the alien Ephus Kennedy. I went to see the man that morning. It looked like some of our boys had already got to his black buggy, reduced as it were to no more than a pile of splintered wood, all banged and shot up. And yet, ducking into his tent, catching him there with his back three-quarter to me, hiding his face, his chest leaned over the prostrate body of none other than the widow Stowe laid up on a big wooden plank, Kennedy's fingers fiddling around in the old lady's mouth, I figured the buggy was no more than an afterthought to this man. And I'd heard all about how he'd put Doc Pinckney out of work in hardly more than a week. People were flocking from all over the county and beyond just to see him. One man was even dragged all the way from Chester and Kennedy cured him of his bum knee. The biggest one I heard was a lame man was carried into this very tent and, 20 minutes later, began the long walk upright back to his great country home. A little croup couldn't be nothing for a man like this.

I coughed, barking a big loud one in spite of myself, when I caught sight of Kennedy's fat fingers in the widow Stowe's mouth, and the fat doctor didn't hardly even move.

"Hello," he said, without turning round, the voice of a Yank if I ever heard one. I barked again. He shushed me quiet. "You will disturb her," he said, not looking back from his task. The devil, Thorpe says, is a Yankee with a cigar in his mouth. And though a big cigar sat clearly there afire in an ashtray at the doctor's back, I figured it could not be very far from the man's lips. I took it all in, trying at the same time not to think of any of it. The doctor had a big fat butt like the one I'd seen on the editor of the Charleston newspaper the time he rode through town. Despite all, I was curious. I held down another cough, then whispered to him, "Whatchoo doing there?" I never been to no doctor but Pinckney, and he was a skinny old runt. But Kennedy wasn't about to answer me. His fingers emerged from Missus Stowe's mouth and he turned round, finally. He picked up his cigar and shoved it into his fat, hairless mouth, gave a cloudy pull through his fingers, which were speckled with blood.

I shuddered. "Hey now!—" I began to protest, seeing the blood, but couldn't get it all out before I broke into a heaving fit and Missus Stowe's eyes flew wide open. She sat up, stiff, a gargled moaning exploding from her body. The fat doctor prized a bloody rag and a brown bottle of something from a side table. He doused the rag, put it under her nose, and she fell asleep again. I coughed on and on.

"Sounds like the whooping cough," Ephus Kennedy said. He wiped his hands and stared at me with those black eyes, a smile turned up on one side of his mouth like he thought the cough was funny but didn't want to commit to that thought for fear of God knows what. My body was bent double, and I was looking up at him, struggling to keep the heaving down. "Just a little croup is all," I wheezed.

"Only children have croup," said the doctor, "technically speaking." I managed to collect myself, stood back up and got fighting mad. I stuck out my poor burning chest like a real soldier. "You calling me a child?" I said. "And what in tarnation have you done to Missus Stowe here?" I racked one then that felt like it was born from my belly.

The doctor came over and patted my back as I coughed on. I let him, I guess, because I couldn't even hardly think in the face of the bombs shooting up from my chest. I then let the fat Yankee lead me, coughing, to a chair on the other side of the tent. A big black kettle sat in front of the chair. He lit a blue fire under it with the flick of some kind of match. "I can help you," he said. Maybe kettle is the wrong word. The thing was a cauldron! It began to steam and smoked up the place immediately. I started to feel a little better. He sat down across the cauldron with something in his hand. Through the steam I could barely make anything out. "Where you come from?" I asked. He stuck the thing—it looked like maybe an old craggy pine branch—he stuck it in the cauldron and stirred round and round like an old witch. "You hear me?" I said. He didn't answer, just kept stirring and stirring and the tent got hotter and I was sweating like a cavalry horse in midsummer. Thing was, I had no urge to cough at all. Meantime, something strange was going on with that doctor. I looked up and his head elongated into that of a gargantuan yard chicken. His beak snapped and I heard him ask me was I feeling better. I said by Christ I was and got up to go, but he shoved a talon my way through the smoke and pulled me back down into my chair with an immense pressure on my left shoulder. He clucked something like you'd hear from a duck now, and then I watched that head turn back to the same fatfaced doctor's. I stood up and demanded he tell me where he was from. "And what the hell is in that damned pot?" I said. He stayed in his chair and I watched him go all bird on me again. He began clucking some madness about how he came from up in the sky, how he just flew down. His beak was moving but wasn't really matching up with his words. "But chickens can't fly," I told the monster. He changed back to the doctor almost instantaneously and stood tall from his chair. "You will be well in a matter of days. Just go home and lie down. Get plenty of rest. You will be well." He turned something under the kettle, cauldron, whatever. The fire went out. The smoky air cleared. I took a look at the widow Stowe with her mouth all wide open, then back to the fat man, chicken. I got scared. I took off running and did not stop until I hit town, gasping for breath, the croup back in full force. Doc Pinckney happened to be by the general store where I stopped, wheezing and promptly passing out cold on the old wooden steps there. Pinckney woke me with three slaps across my face, he said. I say "he said" because I could hardly remember what had happened, but that didn't last. "Got you a case of the croup, huh?" the Doc said. "Only thing for that is a cup of goat's milk and a handful of blackberries a day."

So first thing when I got home I went out back of my shack and tried my hand at my goat. She laid a tough kick in my shin before I even got a hand around her teat, though, so I hobbled back to the house, sat down on the front porch and started crying and coughing at the pure madness of it. I haven't cried like that in years.

At the meeting, Thorpe stood back atop the stump and demanded that I pull myself out of the dirt. "Get up, Sampson!" he hollered. I coughed my way to my feet, the boys laughing around me. "Get home!" Thorpe said. "You're sick and you're going to infect us all, by Christ. Are you playing the devil Kennedy's game?" I made it clear that I was not, and that I'd like to stay. After some pleading, and a whole lot of coughing, my request was granted.

And Thorpe riled everyone up good. That night we all met up again. We took the byroad around town in a pack, set upon that chickenheaded man's tent and tore it to shreds. Problem was, he wasn't there. Plus I was down about it. By then, I really was starting to feel well. That croup I'd carried round for weeks now was lifting straight out of my chest. Maybe fat Kennedy had something. I was torn, truly: Kill a chickenhead Yankee from the sky? Or go on, risk losing my buddies and being branded a traitor.

Like to put a lid on my crisis, once the wrecking of the tent was done, two more torches were lit and Thorpe started in with his sermonizing. He jumped atop the same wood plank Missus Stowe had been laid out on, his fist raised high. "Brothers, Southerners united! Something truly wonderful has been achieved this night! We are united as one in our repelling of the heartless white menace, the Yankee. But it don't end here. The devil is obviously not in our grasp, not here…" I was damn near about to cry listening to the man in his holy gray uniform, knowing my allegiance was off, but then a great bird swooped out of the dark sky, snatched Charlie Crawford by the neck and carried him, screaming, away into the air. "That's him," I whispered at Thorpe's neck. "That's that chickenhead bastard." Thorpe apparently didn't hear me, stood stock still, wide-eyed and just plain scared.

And that fat doctor-chicken came back and took one after another of us, even after we'd got smart and out of the clear. By the end, only me and Thorpe were left, and the doctor came after us into the woods. He got Thorpe's uniform coat when he came swooping down from a tree, but in the end we prevailed. We heard a shot ring out of the dark and cautiously followed its report, finding the fat doctor wheezing for breath against the trunk of an old oak, an old pistol that looked to be one of our own held pointed to his face. "You got me," the doctor said, and Oglethorpe pointed to the man's leg, all the while training his gun on his chest.

But it seemed to me he'd shot himself. I watched in horror as the man began to change, his body now shuddering, contorting violently and his face elongating into a kind of fleshy beak. Thorpe fired a shot that missed, and he ducked behind a tree to reload—as did I—as another shot rang out. The sounds coming from Kennedy's metamorphosis had stopped, and we looked to see that the doctor had shot himself in the face like to stop the change. "Nice shot," I muttered, for though I may have previously owed the man for my cure, that wasn't near enough payment for 20 dead.

The Yorkville Donkey Floggers With Golden Riding Sticks, needless to say, didn't meet again. It didn't so much matter, as by the next year Wade Hampton had become governor and saved us all from the Yankee menace. I got a bad sick after that, but it was something else. That croup never did come back.

IT WAS AN INTERESTING CHOICE OF BEDTIME STORY for a couple preteens. It never fully registered with my brother, who always conked out before the gruesome ending, but I forever remained awake, tantalized at the death not of any of Thorpe and Colquitt's men, but of the doctor, the "gargantuan yard chicken," who must have held a divine power like a cartoon, I thought. Pop permitted no questions, though, so I was left to my own devices in computing the details later. My mother helped in this regard. What Pop didn't tell us was of Colquitt's true end. He went crazy, my mother told, was convinced he was a chicken himself; and in the end he would commit suicide. It's never been clear to me whether Kennedy was even a shred real or if Pop just made the whole thing up.

In a moment of whimsy, watching the television some weeks on, after the Trade Center attacks and witnessing the shit-eating president's repeated invocations of the rhetoric of good and evil and religion in general during his PR stunts for the new war on terrorism, I thought that he again had it all wrong, that my ancestor Colquitt had witnessed that old bullshit Rapture, the escapist warping of the return of Christ borne up by stump preachers fully formed from the wreckage of our United States after the Civil War, in the chickenheaded Yankee doctor, a Christ who had I guess found no faithful worthy of carrying back with him, upward. I guffawed at the roaring television. Ephus Kennedy came down and realized that all had gone wrong, and rather than persist in killing the far-gone heathens or persuading the doubtful, he had a change of heart, shot himself in the face to release his divinity, rid himself of his earthly body. And we humans were thus all left behind to wallow in the sticky filth of our corruption, sons and daughters of that damnation.

I steeled myself for the winter. I watched the global aftermath of the U.S. attacks with the detachment of an alley rat. Besides, other things would prove more pressing.

4 Thursday, March 30

NOVA CAPONE IS DEAD

U.S. sez, "Ain't we heard that one before..."

RIO DE JANEIRO, BRAZIL—International gangster and alleged terrorist Nova Capone was reported dead today, killed during a failed hijacking of a cargo ship carrying pharmaceuticals from Capetown to Ri[o de] Janeiro. U.S. authoriti[es] failed to issue a state[ment]

Capone wa[s]

A.H.

SOME DESERVE TO DIE. I'VE KILLED; THE MAN WAS A no-bit crook, a politician who never saw it coming. He'd had the nerve to mess with my man, the Brazilian… Actually, I've no idea if he's even a true Brazilian or of some other Latin American nationality, not that it really matters: the last time I heard word from Nova Capone he was atop a stage amid beats and I was with him blasting air through my trumpet to a crowd of 2,000 humans packed tight into a ramshackle Sao Paolo ghetto. Otherwise, Nova spoke to me through a Chicago middleman, a bearded white boy named Caliente I knew to be a piece with what I call the *whip junket,* a network of bearded white boys in Chicago apartments with curiously Latino affectations they displayed with no head whatsoever, but all the no-fashion flair a body could muster, hence the *whip*. Or maybe the term signified my own mental combination of *white* and *wop,* which makes as little sense in this case as did they. The messengers cut an insane picture, but so very natural was their machismo posturing that it became something beyond the real. The boys were very comfortable in their short boots, Texas-style and steel-toed. I fucking loved them for it.

Caliente, whose name was once something considerably simpler like Charlie or Edgar, I'm sure, was my old messenger from Nova, and as such he facilitated the little things I'd done for the man over the years. I put Nova up in my spot in Chicago whenever he came through with his act: breakbeats, acid, house, the man did it all. I had him open for me at more than a few of my shows in the early days. He flew me and my brothers down to Brazil and the world spread out in front of me, a mass undulation of human sex, wide-open mouths, sweet hands flinging ragged flowers pulled from cracks in the pavement up to the stage. A rose I remember lodged in the bell of my trumpet. It was beautiful.

Nova got huge, independently. After the show that night we talked into the dawn, drinking wine in his little apartment. He told me his plan. While he toured the world, the Robin Hood was setting up contacts and a tight ring that operated globally, maybe a kind of "terror network" to use the parlance of the U.S. government, but in Nova's case inexorably and incontrovertibly directed toward the good of the common people. Abstract and pure good, none of this pseudo-religious huckster rhetoric you get from the Rapture's mad proselytizers in the broadcast media of late. Nova Capone has reclaimed the noble and rhetoric-free quality of action for himself. Financing the endeavor on his record sales (Nova is worldwide, I'm saying, from Timbuktu to Kalamazoo), he digs mostly in patent fraud and hijackings or, rather, the simple and unverifiable redirecting of U.S.- or Europe-bound ships carrying pharmaceutical cargo or food. He docks them in places that actually might need the shit—worldwide, like I said, from South American ghettos and rural wastelands to lower Africa and lower Alabama. On his crew there are ship captains, muggers, wives, lobbyists, marijuana farmers, chemists, materials scientists and otherwise technologists, complicit musicians like myself.

Picture a world map on a wall in an auditorium and little blinking lights flaring supernova and going dark in the middle of the Atlantic; Nova's death has been reported countless times, though I've no doubt he's still alive, still working it, still fighting.

QUITE SOME TIME AGO, AFTER MY BRAZIL SHOW, a big delivery came to Chicago care of certain of Nova's other contacts in the south-side projects; a hefty bit of AIDS-related pharma cargo slipped and was lost somewhere on the Mississippi-Chicago railway line. An alderman on the southwest side got word of the hijacked shipment and intervened, managing to broker a cooked-up series of narcotics distribution charges for a great many of Nova's Chicago boys, federals locating and seizing the already once-seized cargo and the alderman then, in a vulgar display of power for someone of his ultimate insignificance, arranging to have it sold back to its rightful owner, a hefty profit to top it all for himself. Amazingly, the man made it work; he was a Chicago gangster of the first rate, of the type that runs the city to this day. I watched from behind the scenes the shackling of one after another of our hardworking boys, and I felt the sorrow and vengeance rattling in my bones, felt that my time to act would come.

I waited. Two weeks after the last of the trials, I was in my apartment blowing on the trumpet, getting ready for a show out in Burnham Park scheduled for the following day, when Caliente showed up in black jumpsuit pants and a T-shirt, those low-rise cowboy boots, the black mustache on his white face cut down to a thin line just above his lip. "The time has come, my friend," he said. I took his directive and snooped down to the alderman's home that night; he was purportedly out with a woman who was not his wife, Caliente had said, and would be returning home quite alone, as was his normal rota on these nights. I waited, propped up against a big oak on the little tree-lined street where he lived. Promptly at 9PM his Mercedes pulled up and I strode in front of the car. The man shoved the brake and the big sedan came to an immediate halt. "Sorry," I said. He nodded. "Hey," I said, moving slowly around to his side of the car, "you don't by chance know how to get to—" and it was as quick as that. I had my hand on the knife in the pocket of a workman's jacket Caliente had given me to wear. The alderman played cool, waited it all out just a little annoyed at this odd black man standing in front of him, nodding to my aborted question like he had accepted my deception for what it was, but didn't have the will to escape what he might have seen somewhere in that bloated head of his as his deserved fate. He didn't even blink at the flash of the knife, and I hit his jugular and throat before he could really bother with moving his foot from brake to gas. He began to gag, choking on the blood that spurted in long arcs up into the windshield. His foot slid off the brake, and the automatic transmission eased the car forward into a tree by the curb, the very tree I'd been hiding behind not 30 seconds prior. Just before expiring, finally, the man gurgled a little and turned his panicked eyes to my own, where they suddenly took on a certain resigned quality, near peaceful, corners droopy and wet and a little happy even, alive. He then leaned, straining, toward the window and gurgled what sounded like "Et tu, hipster?" like he'd been cooped up for days with Shakespeare and this was all he could think of. I looked down at my clothes, the navy blue gas-station attendant's jacket, my boots, corduroys, and I laughed high and loud. He collapsed. I reached into the car, turned the ignition back, still laughing, shut the lights and moved back north toward home.

And it was done. It was quite a time ago. I panicked a little while after it and moved my brothers back down home to SC—my mother was dead, and I felt like I needed to be there, which was true, but mostly I wanted my brothers out of harm's way in case the trail of investigation that ensued led back to me, which it didn't. I'd be back to Chicago.

Nova Capone gave up on the United States. He's wanted by the government, of course, all governments, deemed a pariah by the international will to the terrorist label. Those here in the States who would benefit from his particular style of philanthropy are too stupid anyway to filter through the larger media's dead-dog complicity in the "war on terrorism." The rest of the place is too busy with making money and voting big-money hawks back into office to even hear the words Nova and Capone without conjuring the benevolent yet terrific image of the face of that nutcase bin Laden, too busy to ever bother listening to the very real actions of Nova's network itself. Only his beats live on, maybe, among the hipsters and ghetto artists camped in the country's cities, though his music is, officially, banned. I often wonder whether we'll meet again in the brilliant city whine.

Bobby

BOBBY SHOT HIS MAMA. THEY PUT HIM IN THIS HOLE in the wall, behind these bars with a clipped view of the darkened tower. The big lights shine in from the tower. Seems like rats ought to live out there. I haven't been out this hole in a long time, so I haven't seen them; but I know they're there.

Mr. Albert is here. He's got his little metal bottle, and again and again like always a little note shoved in the chest pocket of his gingham. Mr. guard bangs open the bars and helps old Mr. Albert bring the table here into the hole. They've got each a side of it, a table for me and Mr. Albert. A little table. Not much room in here. —Say, Mr. Jeremiah guard, sir, I says. Can't I just this once sit in the chair? It's so damned small in here I have to sit on the toilet, and Mr. Albert gets a chair like all the time.

I don't know when they will let me out of here.

Mr. Albert and Jeremiah, who don't say nothing, they have to turn the table up and sideways to get it through the open space in the bars. The light on the tower gives me a headache, shining in all day and night, night and day. Bobby's ass goes cold on the toilet.

—Howdy Bobby, says Mr. Albert. He unbuttons the second button of his gingham. He's a hairy son of a bitch. A big V of hair all up his neck. He folds out the table legs and sets the top level, leaning way over it and that big V is inches from my face. I lean way back away up and my head cracks the cinderblock wall. My ass is cold here already.

—Mr. Albert, I says.

Mr. Albert turns back, digs in his pants pocket and hands the guard a 20 bill. I think it's a 20 bill. Bobby's Papa's a rich old man, got money and money more. I haven't seen him for some damn time now. Nor Mama. I shot her.

SOME PEOPLE IN HERE CALL ME CRAZY WHEN THEY catch me sticking my fingers in their beans. I love lima beans like Thorpe Storm does women. Get yer'n, they say. Or: muthafuck goddamn sheeit, which is a favorite of the black ones. You'd think none of any of the bastards, white or black, could talk more than a few words, not like Bobby. I got a million.

—What did Mr. Albert say there? I says.

Or: —You've got that same damned gingham you always wear. Can't you afford a new shirt?

Or: —How long till I get out?

I says them all, and Mr. Albert's got his elbows on the table. He peers into me like he's waiting for something.

Mr. Albert sits over the brown vinyl-top table with his eyes all open and big and blue, like mine.

The guard bangs the gate shut.

—So? says Mr. Albert.

—What? Bobby says.

—I asked you a question, says Mr. Albert.

—My ass is cold here, Mr. Albert, Bobby says. Real cold. You got that chair over there, but the water in the toilet is cold.

It's got a seat, thankfully, but no top lid to sit on.

WHEN I WAS A KID AND DIDN'T HAVE NO WHISKEY LIKE Mr. Albert's gone pour me now from his little metal bottle, I used to like his wife. I remember that, a sweet piece with long red hair and big boobs. She used to take my hair when I was shorter and it was a whole lot longer and put it up in all these braids out in front of Mr. Albert's trailer. It was always muddy out there, like a swamp or something. I'd head there after school, cause I always did hate heading home with my Mama in there in her little porch office screaming at somebody on the phone, always screaming, unless Billy came and got me and we went where-the-hell-ever, like the time at that old junked-up place by my friend Jared's grandee where Billy got him a new jacket. We came home and Papa was drunk at the table. Nothing strange about that, really, but I asked for some more milk and he went to pouring it and the woman, Mama, she distracted him and so he kept on pouring. I was drinking out of a little glass for orange juice or apple juice, or milk, and when the milk hit the top my brother Billy started to cursing. Mama had Papa in the eyelock and he just kept pouring into my glass, the milk running over and the white spreading out over the table, spreading around all the dishes with the creamed corn and the country steak and greens and everything and then spilling in a trickle off the side between me and him. Billy screamed a curse and threw his napkin at Papa, who seemed to wake up at the sight of that flimsy paper thing fluttering like a bird in the drafty old house. I remember that, the little napkin floating down to the floor and Papa stopped pouring. —Oh shit, he says, and then bent down to pick the napkin up from the floor and whacked his head on the corner of our dinner table. Right plop down he goes, sideways to the left, chair and all. I couldn't help but laugh a little, figuring he'd jump right up and laugh it off, but he didn't. Mama and Billy just let him lay there all like he was dead and the milk he poured dripping off the table-edge and onto Papa's face and he was snoring almost with the milk seeping and spitting and dribbling across his nose and the air swooshing wet in and out with a sucking sound and Billy muttering under his breath but continuing on eating like it wasn't nothing, Mama telling him to quit cursing and me to eat, Bobby, eat, Bobby, eat. I couldn't take no more of it after a while and lay down in the bottom of my big closet, my Sunday clothes hung up above me. But that didn't help, I could still hear his snoring through a heating vent in the closet by my head. It was a sort of nice thing, really, and I fell asleep to it. I dreamed I was a bird, a baby bird with steely teeth for killing.

MAMA RAN FOR MAYOR ONCE, BEFORE I SHOT HER. And Papa was a man named Johnny who all the kids knew had money. Everybody, old folks too. I loved the man. He didn't like my records. He put GN'R and the Crüe and *Night Songs* and *Operation Mindcrime* and some others all in a bag in my room one night and stomped them into little plastic bits and twisted tape. I sat on my bed and didn't say nothing until it was over. Fuck me, he did it. He did it with his big boot shoes. Brogans, Mr. Albert would call them.

Mr. Albert's wife had good records, too. She set up the speakers in the window of their trailer so they played out into the mud where I was, my hair braided up like Medusa. She kept the braids clipped together on their ends with these orangey pins from the clothesline. I always thought they looked like alligators.

—Where's Ms. Albert, Mr. Albert? I says. Mr. Albert will not repeat his question. It is a thing with him. He pours the whiskeys, like always and again.

I haven't seen her here, I do say. —Why don't she come with you?

It takes him a couple seconds to look up from the glasses, half full as they are. He's angry.

—I did not come here, he says, very slow, to talk about my poor wife. She's long dead anyhow. Now let's have us a drink here.

Bobby shot Ms. Albert. No, Mr. Albert's wife was no mama at all. She had big boobs and that long red hair and little mousy face to match it. I shot my mother, an old woman with a girly bob haircut at age 40 and some. She was running for mayor and brother Billy had a .45 in his drawer. He pulled it out one night and showed me, ran his hands over it like it was a baby or a hottie and said one of his redneck friends stole it from an uncle. I got the gun and waited, after a school day. So boring. I had learned to do my own hair up in them braids and with my own alligators from the dime store, like my mother called it, though I paid a quarter for them. Papa was nowhere, always nowhere. Billy says he's the rascal, Papa, but he's tied with a leather whip. He told me. He said she did it, tied him up so he couldn't get nowhere without her leave. We sat at the dinner table and she was gone somewhere and Billy was down in Columbia getting learned at the college. Papa caught me smoking that day. He caught me in my room fucking Molly and I had her bent face-first over the edge of the bed, and I was standing behind her, doing her, smelling the sweet pussy smell and toking on a Marlboro—nothing goes better with sex than cigarettes, Billy taught me. Been a long time for that, sure. When you get to the end, and the shock shoots up your legs and you hold your breath, take a big pull on the smoke…whoo!

Papa walks in at that moment and the words out of his mouth were

"When'd you start smoking, boy?" Shit. My room door was closed, but Molly was panting and whining into my pillow, and the door's got a big crack down the middle. I once put my foot hard enough into it. Must have been 15.

Papa sent Molly embarrassed as hell home and then he sat me down at the table and made me smoke cigarettes with him until I was blue in the face. Finished off two packs between the two of us.

—Well, you're a man now, he says, pointing to one of the empty packs. I puked on the spot, well well. Bobby made a man by puking his guts out on the kitchen table. I kinda feel like a little kid all the time with Mr. Albert. He acts like he knows something he ain't telling me. I haven't lived my own, though, locked up in here with nothing to do but watch Mr. Albert pushing his glass my way, like he wants me to drink it too. I don't know why he ever comes, really, but it's regular. They say Papa pays him and the guard to let him do it. Albert meantime says a man deserves his whiskey. Bobby's a man.

—I like the fire it puts in my belly, I says. I down it in a gulp.

Mr. Albert takes the letter from the chest pocket of his gingham and lays it flat on the table. He smoothes it out with his left hand. He pushes it across to me. —You'll read it today, he says. Never do I read a letter less it was from Billy, who don't write no more no way. He don't give a fuck.

—It ain't from your Pop, Mr. Albert says.

—My ass is real cold here, Mr. Albert, I says. And the light out there on the tower it gives me a headache. I can't get away from it ever, less I move way back into the black corner on the side of the hole where Mr. Albert is. I don't tell him this. Albert nudges the letter on the table a little closer. But I do tell him about the rats. —Mr. Albert, I says, did you know that rats live in that tower? Swear it seems like it. They like to crawl up over each other, like Yankees. They pile up on each other in that tower like Yankees in their buildings without porches.

Mr. Albert shakes his head and I laugh. He leans way back in his chair, hands on his head. —Yes, yes I know. Just like Yankees in their cities. Should've never told you nothing about that. Mr. Albert's shaking his head some more, back and forth. It makes me smile. His eyes ain't looking into me like they want something no more.

—Good drink, I says. That's what you always says. Them Yankees don't know how to live.

And Mr. Albert rests his arm over the little flimsy post of my cot.

—Are you gonna read the goddamned letter or not, boy? he says, mad, gingham puffing out every whichway. —Your time is done. You're getting out, for Chrissakes!

I ALWAYS WANTED TO DO HIS WIFE. I GOT CLOSE, TOO. She was done with hanging the laundry up and then we set in the mud by the trailer and the Crüe was playing up in the trailer windows cause Mr. Albert wasn't home. Mr. Albert liked country. I was on my bottom in the mud and Ms. Albert was up on her knees and leaned over the front of my head doing up the first of the braids. Those boobs were pressed into my face. I breathed in the sweaty smell of them and let my hand up under the old white T-shirt she was wearing. I latched onto one like it wasn't nothing for me to do it. She kept on twisting my hair. And so I let my other hand up there, in among the sweat and hot and she kept on twisting and soon enough her breath did start to come in long and slow and hard and I could feel it on the back of my head, hear it in that chest my face and hands was planted in. So I let my left hand down her slick, sweaty stomach and under the belt buckle and down the hair and Ms. Albert's breath started really going then and I hit a spot of wet down there before she did hitch up and laugh and tell little Bobby to cut it out. It's a real shame. There's a black man in a hole next to mine who has a visit from a black lady I've seen once. Poor Ms. Albert. Damn Molly. Papa saw her pretty ass all shining there and all he could think to say is when'd I start smoking.

MY PRICK PEAKS UP LIKE A TEEPEE IN MY BLUE PANTS. But Mr. Albert can't see it. —My ass is cold here, Mr. Albert, I says again. He passes me a pack of Marlboros. I open it, and here the hard prick starts to go soft again until I light one and Molly pops into my head and Mr. Albert is talking, but I can't hear him. I smoke on the cigarette. —What you say there? I says.

Mr. Albert shakes his head again and opens the letter and mutters to himself before he starts to read it out. It's about Robert Lee Jones whose father named him after a famous golfer and general both, so they used to say. I am the Queen of the World! Fucking-A, men! Molly used to say when it was over, she did like it so much, she said. I did too, it's true.

Robert Lee Jones, named for a famous golfer and somebody else, is here and thereby will not further be…or something like that. —They ain't gone let me out, I says.

Albert is saying it, reading it about me, Robert Lee. Bobby.

And like that he rises. —Drink your whiskey, he says. There it is in front of me. —I thought I already drank it, I says. It sits atop the brown card table, brown filtered through brown whiskey and browner, almost blacker, still, and shining in the spotlight from out there, the tower and rats that watches with that big, bright, round alien eye. I pick up the glass and down it just before Jeremiah the guard hurtles back into the frame of the bars, my bars, I hold them when staring into the light, daring it to go off. This is my third whiskey today, a rare thing, really.

The bars bang open, and Mr. Albert walks through into the white-hot light and Bobby can't feel a thing again. My ass is cold. Albert will be back, Mr. Albert says. But I don't want to wait. Up and into the light I go, and hands grab at my shoulders and elbows but the guard he can't stop pure me, yes, out into the light a sparrow with tiger teeth, wings for eyes. I can see you fuckers. I can, Papa. You bright blind fucking rats.

The guard muscles me back to the toilet and Mr. Albert walks on away, shaking his head again. But I can wait, have waited, did wait, and my hair all done up in them braids with orange alligators holding them together at the ends and with the .45 in my hand, hot, cold, the narrow little hallway from the side door and the shadow cut into six by the slats, panes, pain, hot pain in my hand when she walks in and the thing fires, all boom and blast and blood.

WHERE.

HERE.

THE LIGHT IS BRIGHT LIKE THE RATS' TOWER, but the color ain't a bit the same. Nor the cot—this soft thing creaks like God hell. Mr. Albert comes striding through a skinny black space every so often. So-often. Mama used to say it like that.

The light is more yellow like a disease around a black one's eyes. It burns through the lampshade on a little table at the edge of this creaky cot. Mr. Albert wears his favorite gingham, hairy V and all, and comes over to me and lays his hand across my forehead like he ought to be my own Mama. —How you feeling? he says.

Who deserves to die?

Billy says Papa's the rascal but Mama got the shit-end. I haven't talked to him since he told me in a letter.

—Go away, Mr. Albert, I says, go away please and thank you and that shit.

—Whiskey for you, Mr. Albert says, and he stands high, dropping a bottle on the table under the rat light. Windows are for walking out, whiskey, wine, the black women with their ringlet hair and big lips. Mr. Albert disappears through the skinny black space and a door swings back to cover it. I haven't opened a window in years, but I haven't forgotten how. Papa sits someplace he doesn't deserve to be. The windowpane is cold; Bobby's up and outside it in no time. Feels good. Decent. It's colder outside the pane, out in the blackness. The wind blows and sticks the hair on my bare arms up like a porcupine. I wrap my blanket around my head and shoulders and open the whiskey bottle there in the cold, bad cold, is all. Though I recognize the street enough. Take it out to Main and you might get somewhere, maybe to Molly's house, though it's cold for that kind of walk. Might be crazy, me, but stupid no. Heave me in, wind. Mr. Albert's got a hell of a porch for sitting. I might step up to it and have this bottle. I might drink the thing away while I freeze, I do say, rock back in his chair with the window light from the front room shining warm on my back, the blanket wrapped all the way clear to my ears and toes, heel up in a little dent in the upper porch railing. Wind sneaks in the gaps, down under and between my legs, through the cheap sweatsuit pants somebody put on me. Out on the road, there is naught. Nothing. I rock swift and short rocks in the chair, whiskey bottle clutched to my chest.

Hey there, little Bobby, says Mr. Albert. Says me, I don't think you have the time for this. I know he don't. Mr. Albert's wife is dead and he's got nothing but a might-as-well-be-dead kid in his spare bedroom, on his porch, now rocking in his chair with no shoes. Have you seen me in the night, Mr. Albert? Have you seen my head rising and on fire? Have you seen Billy? You have, you told me. Bobby'd love so much to see him, his own brother, his blood and piss and that. This chair don't do it. This whiskey.

Albert

MY MOTHER WAS A CRAZY WHORE, AND MY DADDY, the professor Hank Ledbetter, was forever and ever drunk in the family room at the back of the house. Another woman, a friend of my crazy mother's, would come by for a final winter Friday of bridge and dinner with the two of them and her husband. My mother had been steaming up the windows of the house with her insane violence for days in preparation. In classic Ledbetter, or rather her maiden Hickman, fashion, she held an extreme animosity toward the woman's blue and white polka-dotted dress. Mrs. Ziegler wore it every time she came over. Being like us and poorer than your average soul, in possession of only a few decent dresses, and these bridge-and-dinners being just about the fanciest thing she ever did, the blue and white polka-dotted number was her choice for these little gatherings.

I was ten years old.

After four hours of cheap booze, Mr. and Mrs. Ziegler would leave, and my drunk daddy, on the lonely couch back in the family room, heard no end of my mother's screaming about the dress. The lady wore it over and over again to demean my mother, she figured, like our house wasn't good enough for even a change of clothes once in a while: she's only going to those *Ledbetters'* place...though to have seen the woman even a ten-year-old knew this sort of high-toned narcissism was not the thing going through Mrs. Ziegler's mind. Her nose sprung out from her face two feet if an inch, and she was by-God ugly and humble for the fact, walked with her head down like a dog. And though the bridge nights were a long-standing tradition spearheaded by my daddy and Mr. Ziegler, Professor Hank grew weary of the constant litany my mother spat his way. By that time in his life all he wanted was to be allowed to get drunk on the couch in front of the old tube without her standing over him with that bobbed black hair swinging wildly and the veins bulging in her neck. It was his idea, he told me, what they did.

That final wet winter Friday my mother banked on Mrs. Ziegler wearing her dress. She banged out to Plej's in the family Buick the Monday prior and got her own, a blue and white polka-dotted number that hung a little higher up her tanned calves than Mrs. Ziegler's, though the pattern was a replica. I watched my mother over the course of the week wearing the dress when she got finished with the dishes from the evening meal, then torturing my little tabby cat Mickey in the corner of the kitchen with a red-hot iron poker from the coal-fired stove. I watched from under the table in our pitiful excuse for a dining room. I won't deny I cried. That cat was mine. And if I never did have a shred of love in my heart, I did understand property. It hurt. Through the legs of a chair, I watched my mother's bare calves framing my wide-eyed Mickey as he clawed and darted and was kicked and burned back into the corner of the kitchen with the red-hot poker, just like a rat.

She kept it up all week long, and I was powerless to do a thing about it. The woman held every awful thing that happened over my head at the time—the atomic bomb, for instance, the communist witch hunt of the 50s and early 60s, my dad's drunks—afraid or just too stupid to suss out the root causes. I was deathly afraid of her. When she was done each night I had to hold Mickey down while she ran and locked herself in her room to change out of the polka-dotted dress. Later, he'd charge anybody he didn't know like an attack dog. But here he was this little tabby cat, lazy and should-be harmless, named after a cartoon mouse. It was almost silly, until that Friday came along. Just as the Zieglers were scheduled to arrive, my crazy Hickman-descended mother grabbed her heaviest iron pot and paraded Mickey beside me and my little cousin Clarence Hickman, both of us sitting on the couch watching, terrified, in the front receiving room, watching as my mother, wearing the polka-dotted dress fresh from a hot-poker session with Mickey the cat, walked into the front hall, poor Mickey tucked upside down under one of her arms and scratching and clawing at her shoulders, hissing wildly, she with her biggest black iron pot under her other arm. She laid the pot upside down over his unruly frame without ceremony, then ran back past me and Clarence and into her room. She emerged moments later in a bright yellow dress and stood stock center of the front hall with her arms akimbo, facing the door.

Mickey was really stuck under that pot. From the couch I watched it between the backs of my mother's calves. The pot bumped, danced, jumped half-inches from the carpet in the front hall. Mickey tried his damnedest to get free, never slamming his head into the underside quite hard enough. The pot jumped high once, and my mother bent down and lovingly patted its upturned black bottom. She raised back up, smoothed out the front of her yellow dress and put her arms back akimbo, fists fastened to her hips. I dared to utter a mild protest. Clarence rolled over with his face down on the couch and began wailing in fits. My mother wheeled around and just pointed at me. Her face took on a character of menace whose intensity I'd never seen. "Don't fuck this up," she said, that outrageous yellow dress glaring there terribly in my eyes like it was ablaze with pure rage. I mewled, but I did not say another word. "And you shut up, Clarence Hickman," she hollered my kid cousin's way. He continued on with his wailing and whimpering.

Soon enough, the Zieglers came knocking, and my mother reached out and opened the door. There she was, Mrs. Ziegler, just ahead of her husband, with her arms outstretched and reaching for my crazy mother's embrace. Her husband reached up to her shoulders and delicately removed the afghan shawl she wore against the wet winter. Mrs. Ziegler smiled wide for my mother, revealing a new set of dentures. "And new teeth!" my mother spat, immediately, as the woman stepped inside the hall. "Coming into my house with new teeth and still wearing that ratty dress!" And Mrs. Ziegler stopped, her smile evening out, and looked down at my mother's foot, which was cranked back to kick at the iron pot for some strange reason laid out there on the floor. Other than that, I can't imagine what went through the poor woman's head in that small moment, though you could see the horrified realization in her eyes. "Look out, lady!" little Clarence called out, and my mother's foot then punted the pot, which crashed into the wall in the hall, and up and out come Mickey, fur burned and matted here and there in the dim light, that which wasn't raised in fright or outrage or whatever it is cats think and feel. Mickey looked up at my crazy mother and seemed to recognize his tormentor there, for he sneered and hissed at the woman in her bright yellow gown, but the alarmed cry of Mrs. Ziegler drew his attention elsewhere. His poor burned head and eyes turned her way and what he saw there, I imagine, was just one thing, and whole lot of them at that, for she was wearing the dress, predictably: polka dots.

MY FATHER WAS A PROFESSOR OF LITERATURE AT THE local college at the time. He was also a drunk, but none of this precludes the fact that the man knew a thing or two about cats. Mickey charged that lady, and it took the combined strength of me and her outraged husband both in the rain and cold to get him unclamped from her leg. I held the beast down out in our front yard, dusk coming on, rain pouring, as the husband piled Mrs. Ziegler into their Plymouth and proceeded to the hospital. When, finally, they were out of sight I let Mickey go and he ran off down the road, even, hissing, like he would catch them. I skulked back into the house and plopped down on the back couch beside my drunk daddy. Ed Sullivan played on the tube. My mother left to deliver the unruly Hickman kid to his own family. "Is it over?" the professor slurred.

"Is what over?" I said.

"Don't get me wrong," he said, head lolling my way and those drunk brown eyes shining in the TV's glow. "I don't typically condone the torturing of animals, but sometimes to get a little peace one's got to take extreme measures."

I didn't follow much, and told him so, and then he explained how he'd told the crazy woman just how to get back at Mrs. Ziegler and her polka dots. And, later, maybe two years on, my wily daddy would use this act, the training of the quite possibly first-ever housecat attack unit, as proof of the crazy lady's insanity when they divorced. My mother objected, of course, saying it was his own idea, but nobody believed her. By then she even looked crazy. Her hair had got more wiry, her eyes shifty and with a sadistic sheen to them. Plus, she didn't think to ask me to testify, I guess. And if she did I don't think I'd have agreed to it, truthfully. Neither of them, father nor mother, was worth even their decrepit clothes, and my mind was better for being rid of them.

Mickey lived another ten years and I took him with me when I moved to the trailer with my high-school sweetheart Liz. Polka dots were quite the fashion by then. And that trailer was never robbed, long as Mickey was there. I am pure grateful to the beast's soul to this day.

Hickman

CLARENCE HICKMAN PICKED UP THE TRUCK AT eight, a 16-foot cutaway box unit, yellow as a snake. Bouncing it back along I-85 toward his north Charlotte home, his mind keen on the canary exterior of the ghastly thing, he could call up no word for the impulse that would compel a man to go with the particular company he'd rented it from—every one of their trucks blazed this sickly yellow—but *desperation,* maybe, for it was the only one that would allow him the wiggle room. Hickman was down, see. Credit shot. He'd maxed three cards to the tune of $30,000 over the course of ten years. At the end of it, marketers were overloading his poor white telephone with ringing offers of even more credit. Hickman, all the while, normally spent the daytime hours hiding out in his bathroom from the stiff-shirt creditors and ragged repo men banging on his front door.

He was going to Lamar Avenue in Memphis, a destination otherwise unknown except to the minds of the three Memphis hippies he would shack up with. Sarah, the only lady of the trio, played the ukulele and gave Hickman his new name. Man John, she said. "You'll be him." The story went: a Kentucky Presbyterian minister gone crazy on speedballs, come down to Lamar Avenue for his own personal Rapture. "Speedballs?" Hickman said, incredulous. "Yeah," Sarah said, magnificently cocksure, her near-dreadlock braids jumping around with her head. She pulled a plastic baggie full of little blue pills from a nearly invisible pocket in her flower-print house-dress. From that point on, all was unclear.

But for the plan. It'd crystallized at that moment, and Hickman would not forget it. He'd been out with his only pal Fred, a man in a condition similar to his own, out of work, money, love, etc, the night he met the three: Sarah and her dudes Mick and Mike, inscrutable loggerheads with big beards and gruff accents who, the whole time they hung around at Fred's place, passed a joint and muttered lyrics to Rolling Stones songs, mostly the later period stuff, "Honky Tonk Women" on to *Steel Wheels*, etc. Fred went on at length about the U.S. government, the president and his cronies who, he said, believed so hard in the Second Coming it seemed they'd just decided to push it along a bit. For the Rapture is what it is, Fred said. Complete and utter destruction. And these politicians really believed they were on the right end of it.

Fred pulled a bumper sticker from the college-boy shoulder bag he always carried around. He showed the thing around the coffee table in the center of the group.

CAUTION: IN CASE OF RAPTURE THIS CAR WILL BE UNMANNED

Mick and Mike nodded, Mike pulling hard on the joint. Sarah laughed her high and wild cackle. Hickman wondered aloud where Fred got the thing.

"There's a man down around the Circuit City strip mall on South Boulevard's selling them out of a shopping cart, 25 cent apiece," Fred said.

Hickman drove down the next day and consulted with the bum himself, bought his own copy of the sticker there and figured he'd put it in the front window of his little home, where it might make just enough sense to scare off the white-collar collection men, where it'd evoke a twinge of sympathy in the hearts of the bruiser repo guys as well. He placed it in the window when he got home, where it remained an instrument of his salvation.

And yet it was the two loggerheads, Mick and Mike, ultimately, and the lady Sarah in particular, he hoped to make the whole. He had a promise from a doped-up hippie, a woman at that, given to him while he was tanked on near half a liter of Jack Daniel's and those mysterious blue pills. He had an address scratched on a piece of paper. Man John! 'Twas beautiful, he thought. The bright godawful chicken-yellow truck would come damned close to getting him there, he hoped.

WIND BLEW IN CIRCLES IN THE CAB ON THE FREEWAY home, weather sunny and bright for a muggy Charlotte August. The rains come soon, the hurricanes. *Give me hell and high water to hide under,* Hickman thought, *a snorkel to breathe through,* but then again…

Hickman's soaked mind continued on, he'd not have to deal with any of it in Memphis, no more coastal thundercrackers come up with gale winds and flooding his basement, no creditors. Memphis, the high side of the great river, glittering with crack whores, abandoned industrial space where one could take shelter from the stock market. The worst would be the heat, though. Hickman swabbed his forehead with his checkered handkerchief just thinking about it. He took the box truck up 85, blazed to Harris Boulevard and off, pulling the yellow dog home.

Hickman was down, but not so wrecked that he'd hocked his black paint. He'd used it on the walls of his front sitting room. The room could be black as night at midday—he loved it. Late he'd turn off the lights and chain-smoke and sip whiskey for an hour before bed. He called it the headsweep. Sleep triumphed, sans dreams, beautiful and radiant rest. In the morning in the black of the den, he'd sit again for hours and get pumped with anger at the pronouncements of doom spewing from his radio, announcements of things whose meanings were vague to him, things like "civil liberties" being curtailed, or in the case of "precision-guided bombs" the exact opposite: their ultimate proliferation and destructive use somehow presented as humanitarian effort. He could only shake his fist into the air of his apartment. Which he did, morning after morning, screaming back at the radio, never a bottle more than two feet away, though...*Monkey turds! Hog innards!*

Hickman stood off his driveway by the yellow truck, squinting into the summer sun falling on its canary flank, whiskey bottle half full in his right hand, the corners of his mouth screwed up in awe of the ghastly sight. The sun hit the paint and sent the whole of the apparition screaming upward for the clear benefit of GPS satellites, monitors. Chicken-shit, Chinese, down and out in the Mission, alcoholic, jaundiced, three beers and hooked on a hooker. "We get you places." The box told him this. What this thing needed was a blot. Who would go anywhere in it? Hickman ran inside his house, emerging again with a housepainter's brush and a can of Sherman-Williams black for the slogan.

WE GET YOU PLACES

With a generous dip and a long sweep of his arm he obliterated it, the excess paint trailing down the side of the box. A sight better now, he thought, standing back to appraise his handiwork. Night called, rushed him onward. He conjured the glowing tip of his cigarette in his dark front room, thick, aromatic clouds of smoke around him. A damn sight better, he figured, this black swatch, swath, whatever…before dipping the brush again and proceeding to cover the entirety of the box with the black paint. It took him over an hour to really get the yellow gone, and when he was done he was hot and tired and almost totally smashed with drink but worked straight through the paint fumes (now enveloping his entire side yard and house) to fill the truck with his meager belongings. The box stood through it all, deep black and shimmering wet in the sunlight. Night in day. Black in white. Perhaps it's a symbol of racial harmony, he figured, staring at the deep absence of color with a reverence normally reserved for, say, the sun; a curious antidote to racist Charlotte, racist Memphis to which he would maneuver the thing. He pulled hard on the whiskey bottle and relished the hot cold burn as it went down.

Did Hickman believe in the Rapture? By Christ, did he? He'd thought about it these past weeks, concluding that he did, believe. Consequently, not much mattered, really. Rapture awaited. Godawful violence. Jesus would come among bombs, fire in the sky. All would end. No, he wasn't quite dumb enough to think himself among those who would be carried upward. Hell was his to be had, he thought, eyes aimed into a cloudless sky. Besides, heaven was no doubt boredom and drudgery, no whiskey, no easy women, if he went by his own experience, as these women were, at best, whores, and at worst the most evil, conniving group of people on the planet. He met each of his three ex-wives for the first time in the sack, essentially. His second, Esrey, a skinny gem of a hick, laid him up care of a hired thug, a man built like a college football star who gave Hickman the beating of his life. While thrashing him, the man said he was on a mission from Esrey. Told Hickman right to his face. This turned out to be part of her very own instructions, right there in the payment: *tell him I sent you.* Broke each eye socket in three places, nose, jaw. Terrible violence, godawful. Esrey for sure would burn, and so would he.

HICKMAN FELT AS IF HE WERE MOVING HIS ENTIRE house, the sweat was so profuse. He left the phone and little answer machine plugged into the wall socket until the very last, thinking maybe he'd call Fred and tell him good-bye, at least, but he decided against it. The contraption must have rung five different times in the two hours it took him to finish. Messages from creditors blared the distorted sound track to his final trip into the place before he could take no more and pulled the answer machine from the wall socket and stomped it into oblivion, stuffing the last, tangled remnants of the tape itself into a hip pocket and clearing out, leaving the plastic parts of pulverized machine as the last vestige of himself here. Impersonal, yes, and untraceable were it not for the dead skin that floats in the air as dust and coats every single surface: fingerprints, DNA, technology...but for them he had never been there. Hickman thought hard, receiver and cradle of the little white phone tucked now under his arm there in the sun on his little porch step. He pulled from the bottle, draining the last of it.

Cars whizzed by on Harris with people in them inscrutable and reckless. But for them he had never been here. He smiled into the sunlight.

Turning once more back to the house, he caught sight of the bumper sticker advertising holiness propped in the front window. And he laughed. He laughed so very hard the phone popped from under his arm and busted apart on the step. The sticker had saved him these last weeks. It would save him yet, he figured. But for it, he had never been anywhere. He imagined the looks on their faces, the creditors, the cops who would undoubtedly come when someone missed something he had, when they saw the sticker there not stuck but propped in the window, his house an empty coupe with a straight six under the hood and left there idling lonely and silent. The men would be positively horrified, he was certain, at having missed the heavenly party.

THE SIGHT AND PAINT STENCH OF THE SHINY BLACK box on the highway was a horror to motorists for miles. People sped to get by it. Hickman, of course, would race them until he hit the rental's governor at 65 and had to back off. A cop got on his tail, lights ablaze, 30 minutes down the road and he dodged it in Blacksburg by speeding up an exit, running the red light, and topping a hill before turning off into a truck wash meant for 18-wheelers; the black beast emerged smudged and battered, the yellow now peaking through as a vague orange/grey.

He stood back and swayed, appraising the mottled side of the box on the paved parking lot's hillside. It wouldn't do.

He yelled out to the two service station attendants milling about slack-jawed by the pumps, "Got any spray paint in there?" They ogled the box while he pierced their listless bodies through with his stare. "What's the matter?" he said. "Ain't you never seen a yellow truck?"

"That ain't yellow, mister," one muttered as Hickman passed on his way into the store. "More like green."

"Mauve, ain't it?" said the other.

Hickman purchased a can of black and rushed back out and covered as much as he could, getting mostly just the insignia, the hideous slogan that had announced itself after the water hit it. The attendants slumped against the pumps and elbowed each other, muttering and laughing the whole way through it. Hickman flung the can at them when he was done, and the two scrambled after it as it rolled down the sloped lot. He pulled away in the heat, the box of the truck now resembling a jaundiced Dalmatian. He could've hoped for better. He sucked on the hot wind blowing through the cab, the smell of the paint on his upper lip and hands, the ubiquity of the stench. He cracked a new bottle and drank. This is what it must be like, he thought, breaking the governor and on to 90 mph through Asheville, down an Appalachian hill and up again, doing 80 now but still clicking along, sweating, this must be it, this must be, thinking as the clouds parted up the side of the great mountain and let him on through, still toward his end.

YOU WIN SOME, LOSE SOME,
AND WRECK SOME.

—Dale Earnhardt

WHEN ARIÉL CAMINOS WAS JUST A YEAR OLD, HIS father fled, leaving him and his mother to rot in a cave among the mountains and desert scrub 30 and some miles south of the Texas border. After a certain time in the dark, the Mother carried wailing Ariél into the light and then two miles to the nearest road. She started walking north. It was the trail the banditos took in the days of old, nowadays that of the drug dealers and other criminals on their way to the heathen's promised land to the north, where palaces of gold and black crude sprouted clear from the dirt, where disreputable men drove big white Plymouths and Cadillacs.

Two days later, her knees buckling under the little boy's weight, the Mother decided she'd had enough of sweating and the boy's crying; she used the only change she had to call in a favor. Her sister owed her for leaving, she figured. Her sister was fat and happy in the promised land herself, but farther west, where women were fanned silly and fed by jowly white men. Mother and son arrived at a pay phone by the old road, the phone stuck to the side of a power pole long ago left barren of the appropriate wires. Dust circled in mini cyclones around the Mother's feet. She gazed up into the sun to the very top of the pole, the barren wooden cross stuck high and lonesome. She uttered a quick prayer, took the dusty receiver and dropped her change into the machine, holding her breath to hear the crackling dial tone over the whir in her head. She wiped the sweat from the back of her neck and dialed.

Her sister came on the line like it was a routine call, seemingly ignorant of the vast distances between them. Ariél began to cry there in his mother's arms while she talked. Her sister would come through. Wait, she told the Mother. Find shelter and wait. Baby-Ariél wailed, cried the time away and did not stop over the course of days that passed one after the other like cattle as the two holed up in an empty shack on the dusty road a few miles north of the phone. They subsisted on cactus juice, brush fires for warmth in the cool night. Time shot loud with lightning. The sun beamed through cracks in the shack's wooden walls, the interior burning bright to black and back, forth, a creeping disease aware of neither its origin nor destination.

Finally, two large men darkened the doorway on a bright morning. "We are from your sister," one said to the Mother, then placing her and Baby-Ariél in the back of a limo where they gobbled ham sandwiches given to them by the men. They idled quietly past the border patrol. A fine midsummer day, heat shimmering up off the Texas highway beyond their tinted windows, the Mother asked if they'd yet arrived, in quick Spanish, crossing herself repeatedly. The crew-cut heads of the men swiveled back to her as if on a wheel, their sunglasses black to confirm the answer. The baby cried, long and loud.

After a time the two were dropped in an alley in the heart of a city. One of the men handed the Mother an envelope full of greenbacks of large denominations, and the limo peeled off, the Mother and her baby left to fend for themselves in the rabid landscape (gangsters circling, trash piles, bulbous desert rats, outrageous screaming from the window of a house just off the alley). They caught the nearest bus and rode for a good 30 minutes from the city center. They disembarked.

Ariél later dreamt in his crib—in the tiny bungalow her sister's payout afforded the Mother—of cowboys and Indians, men of the law and rangy horse thieves, the walls of the bungalow having been imbued with the sound of the city's television broadcasts. The Mother had picked up the ten-inch tube at a yard sale in town for a buck-fifty. "Ariél!" the Mother chided the boy for the hours spent in front of it. She spoke the Spanish she wanted him so badly to know—but he never understood a bit of it after the advent of the ten-inch television. He dressed in chaps and old vests with faded imitation-gold buttons and sat rapt by old John Wayne flicks, eyes glazed in attention, wet mouth open and drooling. "Ariél!" The Mother went through three rolls of toilet paper a day wiping the spit from his chin. The boy drooled on.

Ariél had grown to a precipice of 5'5" by age 17. His mother would look him up and down from time to time and comment, now in English, that he was a man. Meanwhile, days after school Ariél would forgo the ten-inch television in favor of the antics of one Whitey, who came into town from Bovin way out in the sticks. Midafternoon he'd roll up and unfold his strapping six feet from a yellow VW Beetle, his pristine head of white hair popping from the open door and followed by the shine of the white sequined jumpsuit he wore, an Elvis-inspired number. Neighborhood kids would crowd round, jockeying for position as he doffed his white Stetson and launched into a lassoing demonstration. He'd rope the antenna that shot up from the side of the Beetle with looping circles of his arm. With a magnificent gesture he'd rope the car and, at times, the entire crowd, a gaggle of cackling brown-faced boys and the occasional girl just watching wide-eyed or laughing. Many laughed at the old man Whitey, and when, after a short time and concurrent with the ever-shortening attention spans of the audience members, Whitey's whole routine ceased being funny or compelling or even distracting, they left. Though Ariél always stayed, the last kid on the corner. At age 17, Ariél would clap his hands till they glowed red, then on to a nasty purple, pulsing with his fervor. Whitey took notice. He'd leave Ariél with a tip of his white hat. "Thank you kindly," he'd say, Ariél miming a tip of his own imaginary hat back to him, whistling good-bye, rubbing his hands.

One afternoon the kid clapped so hard the flesh between the thumb and forefinger of his left hand split and began to bleed. Whitey tended to the wound with iodine, wrapped the boy's hand, packed him in the car, and they took off to the site of the Roundup, the dusty vaudeville of a rodeo show Whitey ran out in Bovin. In the past he'd done much the same with 15 or so other now-itinerant cowboys at the place. Ariél started in with directions to his mother's house when he realized Whitey was headed the opposite way, but Whitey waved them off. "Is she expecting you particularly?" he said. Ariél shrugged, for she was not. They bumped down desert roads out of the city.

In a red barn half attached at its pentagonal western flank to a kind of ranch house—the blue paint on its wooden exterior blasted by periodic sandstorms to a ghostly off-white—the cowboys groomed their horses this afternoon, looking up at the noise of the VW rattling in the sun outside the open barn door. Whitey rose from the bug, the boy from its other side. The old man walked around the car, pointing, the men knew, to the rodeo ring, where they played out their cowboy drama for city spectators, well-to-do families down from El Paso and others with nothing to do on summer weekend nights.

Ariél stayed on for dinner, wheat cakes and chorizo fried by Seve, the obese Italian cook for the lot. Ariél could not eat, really, so sick he was with delight, with apprehension, and the men at the table couldn't comprehend the boy's wide eyes, his tight lips, the way the bottom one curled like he'd cry when the old man made to drive him home—though all the men were once just like the kid, hands raw from clapping, minds' eyes on something, dreams they didn't have the language to describe, all now just a kind of dog-eared feeling blown sky high and away by the kicks and dust and sweat of the Roundup.

After that day, the boy planned to join the cowboys, filled himself with momentum toward the end. Ariél never had a girlfriend, got along with neither the rich Mexicans nor the saps poorer than himself. The strangely hip gangbanger boys knew something he didn't want to comprehend, so he'd drifted through high school as with blinders to the rest of his generation shielding his command of the periphery. He fashioned himself a lone ranger. Reaganism was in full swing: strip joints and malls and other trickle-down products like adult video shops and discount variety stores and peepshow theaters and disco bowling alleys had moved into the neighborhood. He figured the bravado and determinism of the western genre to be sincerely a part of the cultural dynamic—people *had* and others *had not* but still really felt they could possibly *get*. Ariél, having finally grown into his brown leather chaps and those gold-buttoned vests, stole a black Stetson and 200 cap pistols from a vendor at a dirty city flea market. He trailed across the school's dusty campus chanting loud and hard about equal rights and other such anathema, telling it like he saw it: through the foggy lens of the television screen, with a high sense of the absurdity of his message thrown in for full pathetic affect (the skies split wide and poured glorious rain, ending a drought and announcing the victory of the candidate). He was elected to the school's open senior student council seat, outstripping all others in the final vote by more than 200 percent.

Perched atop the seat he did relatively little but squirm: the tiny men and women on the council bickered at their meetings about where, for instance, the new Coca-Cola vending machines should be placed and how, in turn, they might get their meager protestations on these placements out to the folks who really controlled the spots—the principals, vice principals, the directors up on the district board. Ariél rarely attended a meeting, but he nonetheless got his main wish: he was warranted a seat on the stage at his graduation. He donned the black cap and gown, draped the student councilman's blue-and-gold sash across his chest, on his hip a holstered cap pistol hidden from the crowd's view; he sat sweating in the end zone of the school's football field under a fiery

June sun through the whole of the proceedings. He gazed out across the black sea of similarly attired students in front of him and up the bleachers in back, where old man Whitey sat next to Ariél's mother, chatting. From the distance of the stage, Ariél could just make out his mother's angry, firmly set jaw, the black slits of her eyes, his mother appearing Whitey's veritable antithesis in a billowing yellow sundress, her long black hair pulled tightly back from her forehead into a thick braid. Whitey's glowing head of hair was likewise up, stuck with pomade in a shiny pompadour. Ariél, sweating rivers under the gown, could see the old man was in persuasive mode—as the anonymous valedictorian droned ineffectually on, Whitey would speak and then nod with a sugar-coated smile toward the Mother and make like to take her arm in his own; the Mother only jerked further away from him in horror. She was hard, hopeful, wanted her son to be a doctor or lawyer, maybe go to Austin to study politics. But as the ceremony wore on, as Ariél rose and jumped from the stage (feeling through the polyester gown for the outline of the little snap-pop pistol at his hip) to take his place in the line of students all preparing for the walk up and across the stage and into the hand of the school's principal, he looked back up to the rear of the bleachers and now spied his mother relenting to something, at the very least—she stood arm-in-arm with the cowboy. The couple behind them pointed and laughed at Whitey's pompadour, his white jumpsuit, and Ariél laughed with them, though here was a man with a gut, he thought, determination, and his mother, by Jesus, fit right there with him. Ariél skipped slowly up the ramp. He made his way across the stage with a slow swagger, the crowd of sitting students now tensing as if in anticipation of his appearance. He stopped just inches shy of the principal, lifted the tail of his black gown to reveal a quick flash of the spurs on his black boots, his brown chaps. He wheeled out the cap gun, turned to face the black sea of students and aimed straight into the sky, the stinging sun, a thunderous whooping rising from the mass of his schoolmates, hats flying prematurely into the air and cap pistols emerging from under more and more gowns, from the purses of members of the audience. The field resounded with the popping. Identical twins from the Roundup—Wesley and Thomas Johns—bent into the center aisle from the rear of the screaming students astride two near-identical black broncos, trailing on a rope behind them a luxurious brown-coat mare with a white diamond between her eyes. They'd ridden all the way from

Bovin. They led the mare up the aisle as graduation caps continued to rise and fall around them. Ariél bowed to the principal—mildly aghast though smiling in his own purple gown—and handed his cap pistol to him, which the principal took and fired as Ariél hopped from the stage onto the brown horse. Wes and Tom led the small procession back the way they'd come, the students with their pistols raised high in salute.

THE ROUNDUP SCRUBS TAUGHT ARIÉL WHEN HE wasn't glued to the very same ten-inch he'd spent his youth drooling over. The box had seen better days—and the signal coming out to Bovin from the city wasn't perfect in the least—but that didn't stop him.

Whitey took Ariél's mother out one night after a month of her son's public training (he developed his chops in front of the crowd, mostly). Whitey sent word of her boy, her man Ariél, who'd taken the reins of the mare and ridden into infamy. They loved him, Whitey told her. The cheering crowds that came out for his runs saw a definite style in the young man's way, when he'd lope the mare in a circle around the ring, flying the rodeo flag, pull up quick and head back the other way now standing full, foot up on the saddle horn and pistol raised to the sky.

If the crowds reacted, chanted the young man's name to the desert winds when he finished, if the Roundup boys professed to never having seen the likes of it, his mother never understood the glory. She died alone in that next summer's heat, the last time Ariél saw her being the day he left, television in tow.

WHITEY OFTEN TOLD THE MEN HE'D NEVER BEEN sick a day in his life. Gathered around a fire nights, they'd laugh, joke with the old man about his apparent immortality. Midseason of the very last of Ariél's 15 years at the Roundup, the old man trundled out one hot, bright Sunday afternoon—Whitey having grown all the more aged and wizened or, you might call it, senile, his ever-thinning white hair falling out in clumps as if mimicking the quick fading of his mind. No one had the heart to advise him, the men falling automatically into their past enthrallment. Besides, he was occasionally lucid. No one paid much attention when he left the barn that afternoon for a short walk in the sand, in his enfeebled state neglecting to reckon the black cloud of a dust storm on the horizon. He ran out with no horse, without any gear but the white undershirt he'd taken to wearing, a pair of jogging shorts, and black Reebok hi-tops without even socks and which, after the dust settled, remained miraculously attached to his feet, his legs jutting up from a sandy embankment and canted at a 45-degree angle to the upslope of the drift. The cowboys gasped, recoiled in horror, standing all lined up behind the one who found him—Ariél. "What now?" he said, and one after the other the men placed their hats solemnly across their chests. Even fat Italian Seve the cook bowed his bald head for a moment, crossed himself and muttered a Hail Mary. "They're pointing east," Ariél said, motioning to the upturn of the old man's legs. Go east, boys! the legs said, or seemed to be saying, go east! Follow my soul! Ariél raised his middle finger to the distance. They all sat in the barn for the remainder of the day and brushed their horses to keep their hands occupied, their minds off the disaster. They couldn't bury him properly, couldn't do anything with the sand out there in the wind. Every attempt at shoveling the stuff away from the gleam of his legs resulted in his seeming to sink further in; the wind would not stop.

Morning in the barn the next day, brushing horses and cleaning and dumping ash from their fires and shoveling unwanted sand out of spaces that couldn't seem to defeat the howling wind that brought it in, the men called their senses from the mundane tasks to a curious roar in the distance. They gathered in murky sunlight outside the black of the open barn door.

"What is it?" Corey said—all 6'5" of greaser leather (he was the gangly James Dean in their cowboy drama)—upon witnessing a dusty-orange plume rising from the horizon like a jet's cloudy aftermath. Corey spat into the dust at his feet, threw on his greaser shades, and adjusted his leather jacket to repeat the question. Ariél emerged, finally. "Sounds like a car," he said. He brought his right hand to his brow to shield his face and eyes from the sun pouring in from the east; they watched the juggernaut come on.

It came to rest just ten feet shy of the men; the car was covered in the sandstorm's dust and dirt, which pockmarked the pavement of the only road to the Roundup for miles, and after the machine came to a halt, the cloud it had kicked up then cast its grit on every member of the group. Ariél pulled a scarf over his nose, his eyelids pinched to a slit watching the driver's side door of the old green Pontiac GTO. The driver cut the machine's mean idle and rose, coughing, from the contraption. "Goddamn!" Corey loped up to the car. "That a '64?" Their visitor slammed the door and began dusting his mirrored aviator sunglasses with the tail of his T-shirt. "That's right, friend," he said. "Been a long drive." Corey backed away then to Ariél's side, nodding appreciatively. The man slid his shades across his nose and now burst into a laugh so violent that Corey couldn't help but to join him. Not a word was said before all of them were clutching their stomachs. All but Ariél, who pulled the scarf down to his neck and asked the man what he wanted here. He did not reply. He turned and took in the dusty landscape behind him. "What's your business here?" Ariél repeated, but the man only attempted to collect himself, further, sauntering up to the small line the men formed. He began to talk on how funny they looked in their leather pants, their vests. But the men's slightly befuddled gazes quickly became scowls, and the new man then jumped back a step, raising his palms. "I just heard about you guys up in El Paso," he said. "Heard the old man died yesterday. It's a shame. Sure would've liked to see you do the show." He looked young, as old as maybe Ariél's 32 years, though it turned out Johnny Jones was much older than that, his long unkempt hair imparting to his face a certain youthfulness the moment you met him; in truth it was as haggard and lined as any of the old team's. Ariél repeated his query like a mantra that day until Jones got around to formally introducing himself, but he wouldn't give up his secret, not yet, not until he'd worked his way on every cowboy at the Roundup. Johnny Jones—the man in the mirrored sunglasses, AC/DC T-shirt, torn-up jeans—could make you forget all about what he was saying, had a way with his talk which set your eyes firmly on your mind's disbelief at what his arms were doing. He'd be telling you about his hometown in South Carolina, and you'd be agreeing him to your own death and destruction while watching hard the snakelike movements of those arms like a man mesmerized by something as dumb as a fish tank. If perhaps Jones ever did amble up to some verifiable point, he'd snap his fingers right by your nose, which would break you from your reverie just in time to catch and feel the weight of whatever he wanted you to take away from the monologue.

After the men had all gone to sleep that night, Jones caught Ariél alone, hypnotized him in the glow of a fire they built outside of the barn in the wind and sand. Jones told of his dead wife, his murderous son.

"I left town a couple months ago, after the trial of my boy Bobby. The kid took his life into his own hands before it was time, I guess, and now he'd spent a good bit of it in the jail and I felt like I was released, a little, wildly sad and elated all at once. I figured I'd head west. I drove hard through the curves and down the hills out of town through a little place called Blacksburg, a high sense on the brain of things gone well, despite all." He smiled, chuckled a little then looked away. "I was paying the prison guards to keep a close, protective eye on the boy, and I'd been sober two weeks now, stone sober and with only the cigarettes to keep me coughing." Jones lit one. "And I lit another then when the highway dropped off onto Main Street in Blacksburg's little crumbling downtown, the few merchants out in the early morn preparing the boot shops and sports stores that pepper Main for Saturday shoppers. This place, old holdout of the Klan and the ghosts of worse, wasn't necessarily a sin, I figured, not like my father used to tell me. No indeed, only a hotbed of the worst the South has to offer.

"I was stopped at the main light on Main, one of the few in the whole town, wanting to believe myself, you see. From the sidewalk to my right came an old man in coveralls rolling an iron lung across the embattled pavement of a side street. I smiled and nodded as he hobbled across in front of the car. I pulled on my smoke, watching him, and the man didn't so much as even look at me until he was almost all the way by, where he stopped up by the left headlight and peered into me with these beady black eyes, smiling to show the world his single front tooth and an enormous outcropping of gum. I nodded and pulled again on the smoke. The light turned green, but the old man hadn't moved on. He pulled his tank to my door and I fought at the urge to gun the motor and peel on out before he had a chance to say his piece. 'Anderson,' the old man wheezed, then, sucking a clean breath from his tank. 'Land in Anderson,' he said. And a great wind kicked up, tunneling through my car's open windows and catching my cigarette from my fingers, whereupon it flew on out to the pavement, rolling across the street. The old emphysemic man scurried after it.

"I forgot him, or tried to anyway, hit I-85, thinking of nothing if not of Cowpens, South Carolina, site of an old Revolutionary War battlefield which I'd seen countless times over the years, the long hill that fell down to trees and the little creek below, all pregnant, full of the mythic blood of fallen compatriots to the great experiments—South Carolina, the Confederacy, America. Placards there talked of the defeat of British regulars by a ragtag group of my own Scots-Irish kin, the hot ancestral blood, see." Ariél did not speak. Jones went on, "A hot day itself, I smoked cigarette after cigarette once I got out of Blacksburg, windows down against the heat and smoke and the coughing that took hold of my chest, which took my mind back to the old man. I'd throw the Marlboro out the window only to light another, lamenting the passing of the generations, the modification of tradition. My Pop, when he was with us, smoked Winstons.

"Cowpens was named for its origins, the beginning of a tradition known more to Yankees and Confederates alike as that of you old Texas cowpokes. From Cowpens were launched some of the first-ever cattle drives of this new world, from Upcountry corral to market down in Charleston in leaner, colonial times, north to the Virginia territory, Philadelphia, New York, even. After the Brits arrived at the place, confronted then by bands of guerrillas, really, under Colonel Dan Morgan, they were routed, and it was long rumored in some of the more fanciful history books that the redcoats were most appalled not by the unconventional hide-and-seek tactics of the men fighting them, which they'd come to recognize at least a little by now, but by the outrageous stench of Hiram Saunders's cow pens even minus the cattle, which had been slaughtered and moved on by the cracker militia in advance of their possible theft by the enemy. I always thought it was a hell of a thing, really—the sacrifice, the stench, the privation—and when I arrived at the old field that day just past 8AM, the little gift shop unmanned this early, I stood atop the hill overlooking the pasture falling into trees by the creek below not even bothering to read those old placards, which I'd memorized anyway—I just imagined the stink, the absolute horror of the foolish British at the nature of the backcountry.

"And then I got back in my car and drove on west toward Atlanta, but long before that was Anderson, as the old man said, west of Greenville off the freeway. 'Land in Anderson.' That old emphysemic oracle clutched his tank and pulled from the mouthpiece when he said it. I was floored, really, couldn't resist the temptation to do it, land. I ran that old roaring GTO aground at a Waffle House in the very town, grinning now at the fat, kindly lady behind the counter. I asked, after a coffee and plate of grease, you know, where'er might be found lodging for the night, I thought I might stay a while. She pointed me down the road to a joint called Hiram's, after all—a roadhouse with a barroom and lodging available for the wayward soul. She'd taken me for such, a trucker maybe, with my scuffed boots and jeans and T-shirt. I didn't correct her, took the advice, rode the hot day through to its end.

"But a sober night in the vicinity of a barroom was too outrageous a proposition. By midnight I'd emptied a fifth of bourbon and, in the morning, I sat up horrified by the pounding in my skull, by the slip of carbon-copied paper on the sale of a tract of land just back a little east of Anderson, my own damn signature slapped at a drunken angle to the black line meant for it. The man who sold it to me—it and an old farmhouse on the property—was this red-faced cracker in a blue-and-white gingham print shirt, a hideous red tie, voice gruff and guttural. I remembered him, barely, but could recall next to nothing the man had actually said other than the property's basics. There in the dark, on that ancient, foreign bed, I was seized by the old alcoholic fear." And here he snapped his fingers and laughed, his body quaking in mock-agony. "But it passed, the fear, with the shakes, and I laughed, eventually, yes, didn't stop laughing until I stood midday on the front steps of the place, fresh bottle in my hand and the deed in my pocket. A fine house, the view from the front porch looking out into the small yard, woods to the left, an old fallow field to the right. Cotton, likely. Long disused. I walked around the side of the house and nearly did recall the man telling me about the creek down the long sloping hill in the back before I saw it with my own eyes. I settled in for the day on a wooden rocking chair on the porch, the chair apparently part of the deal. I drank and, as dusk fell, tossed the empty bottle into the front shrubs. I thought hard of Cowpens, stumbling back behind the house, of all that had brought me here, my life a series of empty bottles lined atop an old peeling white fence and blasted two and three at a time with buckshot as each moment fell away from memory. Man, I got down to the creek and sorta found myself standing in water up to my knees at the very center of a swift current. I lost my footing trying to back up, fell full into the water, which carried me a number of yards before I got my footing back. And I was drunk, near impervious to the elements, so wobbled up to my feet again, licked the clear creek water from my lips and slowly climbed up the bank, dripping, laughing." And Jones laughed hard, again. Ariél shuddered. "I dreamt that night of cattle filling the yard, cattle crossing the creek. A few days, then, passed much the same as the former. I'd found my home, there, among the wild."

Jones talked through the night and waved his arms like a dancing Gypsy, jawing on about a herd of cattle he now supposedly had on that very land in South Carolina, of all places. Ariél listened like he'd never listened before, and the next morning he dressed before the men rose, stood up in the barn's rafters and fired one of his many cap pistols, which brought the heads of the men to attention. Ariél intoned, "Thirty thousand a year, Jones says. Salary. All of you." The men rose from their bags into the morning light. Ariél jumped from his perch and came sailing—chaps billowing—into a large pile of hay. Dust blew up and hung silvery in the sharply angled sunlight pouring through the east-facing barn door where Jones stood, his figure in silhouette, bending over with both arms extended and motioning for the men to rise, which they did, rose and walked and didn't stop until they'd bested the Appalachians, seen a herd of over 500 head spread across fallow fields carpeted with weeds and grass, big oaks, pines.

Ariél jumped from his horse at the precipice of a great, grassy hill overlooking the closest South Carolina came to a ravine; the others stayed mounted behind the top hand as Jones loped down the hill on his white horse into the brilliant herd, merging with it. They'd begun testing their newfound strengths here, running the beasts down Jones's property line, this only for the second time, whooping like mad, like nothing you'd ever heard ("rebel yell," Jones said, "gets them scared up the most," the red-and-white, the few dairy head they had to milk every damn crack of dawn, the brown and the black, all of whom, like Jones, were SC born and bred). They ran the herd down the length of the creek at the bottom a good ten miles to a lake, losing a few along the way and quickly realizing it was wise to be wary of strays. Housecats and dogs and boys would jump barbed-wire fences and crawl through dirt, swim creeks and Upcountry rivers just to catch a sight of the anomalous cowboys frolicking on horseback across the once fertile piedmont: Nancy Miller, the owner of the property adjacent Jones's, would threaten a lawsuit against the man after the second test run. The herd entered a section of her land and left her fat orange cat crushed flat as by an asphalt spreader.

The herd continued to grow as the summer gasped its last breath, cattle spilling over from the fields up to what might be considered a backyard. So extensive was their proliferation that the men often pulled their heads up from sleep in the side yard to curse at their lamentable cohabitation with the beasts—Wesley Johns woke one 3AM with a herd rat staring him down, its beady eyes glinting and nose twitching, at which he screamed like a scared woman, rolled hard away in his bag, in turn scaring the rat enough to leave but rolling hard into the hooves of a big heifer who slept standing there among the boys this evening. She belted a great moo that shot the rest of the crew to their feet. Getting cold this September, the boys now out of their bags, cursing the beast and throwing on their clothes to gather around the docile animal, laying hands upon its flank and pushing with all the might they could muster before, after ten minutes, giving up entirely. They panted themselves back to sleep, and when Jones woke them the next morning with his customary holler out the front door, the heifer stood still there among them, her eyes open, vacant, and slumbering.

They spent occasional nights awake, speculating on the past and future of this man their savior, employer, and what else, a Vietnam vet who felt truly happy for the warring experience. Some said he was absolutely unfazed by the carnage or even the ideals for which he was supposed to have been fighting, a man who spent the subsequent decade whacked out on LSD to come out in the end not with rage, but with something other, vision, however blurred at the edges, vision for great things, great works, some of the men even convincing themselves of the truth in the proposition: Johnny Jones the worker of miracles, the man to move mountains. Ariél did nothing to correct them. At least Jones got them here, the bulk of them thought. Corey was near alone in his vehement denial of Jones's worth for anything other than money. The tall man Corey threw beer cans into the fire at night, threatened momentous if unlikely disruptions: "I'll blow up his goddamned house," essentially, at which point he'd ride off to his woman in Anderson, whom he'd reckoned from a previous era—when an adolescent in Atlanta on mean streets he'd known her, before the advent of any of this nonsense ranching, as he preferred to call it, ranching not for profit but sport. Jones seemed to have no inkling, no knowledge whatsoever, of the machinations behind the beef industry, Corey said, no intention further of doing anything but laying everyone around here and maybe every two days taking milk from some of the dairy cattle and punting it off on a pasteurizing plant up toward Anderson. Corey's cheeks shone a bloody red; he pouted, breached the hard-nosed etiquette of the campfire time and again, shifting uneasily in his leather getup—he continued to wear his Roundup costume in spite of the crew's move. They all did. The truth about the entire group, in fact, had always been the near-astounding lack of irony in the act. They were and would forever be the kind to recommend valor and authenticity before a joke, take it all... Ariél Caminos had grown into a character in a Hollywood western. He preferred the more traditional outfit: chaps and vests and a Mexican sombrero now in a nod toward his anonymous forebear and poor dead mother. Ariél kept Corey skeptical, if regretful, company in his distrust of Jones, regretful for the man paid him well, which Ariél—though fancifully naïve—had come to recognize as important. His trips further east toward Greenville, where the money got him that which fueled his contentment, ran on as happy as sin, nights at a saloon by I-85 called Harry's, where he'd arrive on horseback every second night, take his seat at the bar and drink his due in front of a wide-screen television picking up satellite signals from space. The selection was astounding. The proprietor—Harry, in fact—and his doleful daughter Lula May never tired of laughing at the short cattleman. The man's Texan roots did not even seem, as Harry suspected they ought, to dictate the sense behind a scheme as simple as a hard run off right tackle in a college football game—the instinct for strategy, the underpinning of the will to fight for your life and get one up over the next hill or two. The man at the bar, Ariél, he loved his western pictures, though.

THE NAYSAYERS GOT TANGIBLE EVIDENCE OF THEIR skepticism about Jones a curiously hot night late that September. Merle Jones, Johnny's older cousin, who usually slept in the house on account of his seniority, was set up with the boys for the first time in the side yard. Merle, along with the rest of them, was awakened by a newcomer, a woman, making a loud stomping production of her trip up the front porch steps of the manor before the sensor light there blazed into life and fell full and bright on her red beehive of a hairdo. The tail of her red denim dress swayed slowly in the slight night breeze. She whacked hard on the bull's-head doorknocker and Ariél rolled hard up and out from under his blanket like a scared soldier, hair pricking up with the cold sweat on his arms. He shook the sleep out of his head, spraying with droplets of sweat the rest of the men, up just as quick as the top hand and now flanked behind him, rubbing their eyes against the salty sting of the sweat, likewise the sight—the woman in red's hair seemed afire in the light. "You bastard!" she wailed, whacking again the doorknocker three times in quick succession.

"What in hell—" Wes began before Corey cut him off.

"Damn devil," Corey said.

Johnny's voice came bellowing from the upper story of the house—"Whoa there, woman!" his feet padding then down the stairs from his bedroom. The red woman's whacking increased in intensity at that. Ariél began to creep forward, motioning through the dimness for the men to follow. "Woman, indeed, lads," said 60-year-old Merle, who hobbled with them in full-body white thermal underwear, standing next to Ariél. "And I know just who, too." The men crept forward. "She knows we're here, lads," Merle said, though the woman had not so much as flung her hair their way. "She wants us to see it, the deft humiliation, the pain, dropped like an A-bomb on the head of the poor asshole you all know as Jones, but who is just Johnny, really. Now watch."

All the men but Ariél gawked at Merle, stopped and crouched as they were just shy of a semicircle of light that fell ten feet off the porch. "Watch," Merle repeated, motioning toward the porch, and Ariél looked on with wide eyes to the screaming and wailing woman thinking that maybe this was what he'd missed about Jones, the very thing, the tragic flaw, waiting each and every moment as her white arm rose again from her side, from the red of her dress, and her hand grasped the doorknocker and brought it down, a sound just then, a reverberation through the night like gunfire. She screamed and wailed like Jones had killed her father or husband, whacked down on the knocker again. Johnny Jones yelled a quick and high-pitched stream right back from behind the bolted front door: "What the hell do you want, you cross-eyed old bitch?"

"I'll sue you and your damned beasts," she said.

There in the din, the dark, Merle turned to Ariél. "Yes, lad," he whispered. "Johnny may have met his match, spite of what he told me he would do." The woman's arm rose again and grasped the horns of the doorknocker. Her hand raised it high, palm pressing its chin now and with every scream belting the steel skull's back against the knob on the door. "Yes, lad, I knew she would arrive this night," Merle went on in his characteristic faux-Irish brogue, though he'd spent every moment of his life in this very country; he fit right in with the rest of the men. "Johnny did tell me, too, what he wanted to do with her. Now watch close, boys."

Mid-whack, the door flung open, ripped from the woman's hand. She stumbled a foot forward, then rebounded just in time for Johnny's right arm as it plunged into the porch light and roped her around the waist; the fire-red hive of her hair burst, following her body with a flash, quick, inside—a flapping flourish of the dress's tail was the final remnant of her presence.

"Good goddamn," Ariél said.

"He did it," Merle said. "He knew she was coming," laughing, Merle. "Johnny wanted the house to hisself, he told me. 'You need to practice up for the drive,' he said. Practice for the drive, right. I said what about him? He said he'd do just fine, lads, just fine. 'And so will I,' I said. Then he shook his head a little and motioned me over to him. We were in the den, lads, in there," he pointed to where the woman had just been standing, "just behind the front door. He motioned me over and then put both his hands on my shoulders, looked up at me very curiously, very intently, you might say. Like he was mad or like he was my father or something. 'Trust me,' he said. 'Remember Betty?'" Merle pushed the men then back into the porch's semicircle of light, where they stood with their backs to the porch, the light, Corey muttering a brief "goddamn" to himself, Ariél with his eyes screwed up over the top of Merle's head, the old man pausing long enough for the light to flash out to blackness again, finally, the shadows of the men then merging and seeming to cover the entire landscape themselves. Merle let his shoulders fall slack, pulling a match from his pocket, striking it. "Knew she was coming," Wes Johns said.

"He knew she was coming!" Corey repeated, his greaser pompadour matted up with sleep.

"Indeed," Merle said, "why he put me out in the yard with the rest of you and—" Merle motioned now toward the pasture, the forever unnerving, unearthly rustle and moan shooting now up the grassy incline to them from the herd's mosquito-infested creekside haven below. "You and those filthy animals," he continued. "Somehow knew she would come, lads, somehow—claims she's the spitting image of his dead wife, though the resemblance is little better than passing."

"What was she so mad about?" Ariél interrupted. "What'd Jones do to her?"

"Johnny," Merle said. "What did Johnny do, lad. Killed her cat, essentially. Well, we all did." Merle shook the match dead and told the men of the truth behind the life of their employer, a truth which, at the end of the disclosure, many were regretful for having played audience to, though they sat up through it all with their eyes slit seemingly just on the edge of attention, open only against the sleep that would have deprived them of the knowledge. Johnny was but a refugee from the town of his rearing by choice, old Merle said, like themselves mostly. He was no soldier. Lord only knew if he'd ever hit acid. In the pause that followed he gave a long look toward Ariél. The top hand gazed up at the house in the manner of a disinterested pirate staring into an approaching storm. Inside, Johnny and Ms. Nancy Miller could be heard railing against one another, pots and pans banging around in the night.

Johnny's wife was dead, Merle said, and many thought it the doing of the man Johnny himself, but that was not quite right: many loved the man back in the town as well. "He has money none of you will ever know the likes of, lads," Merle said, "and that is at once blessing and curse, as that old story goes," Jones's fortune earned on the sweat of himself and, mostly, his father, who had long been dead and had left the entirety of his amassed fortune to his only son, who then took what he had and added to it and had two sons, one of whom then decided Johnny's dear wife Betty deserved to die care of his own hands and who might have topped himself and Johnny too were it not for the wife of a friend of Johnny's finding the boy and dead mother before the final offing was ever really in the cards. "Johnny's son is in prison for the killing to this day," Merle told, and the men shook their heads at it, for many of them knew the compulsion—Wesley and Thomas Johns had arrived at Whitey's Roundup in 1975 each just after a similar act, though they'd included both parents in their juvenile rage, the instigation something as untoward as the withholding of a box of saltines or a night out with friends. None really knew the particulars but for the Johnses themselves, who never gave up the full story. Ariél, for all his initial apparent interest in the machinations up in the house, was fast asleep at this point, and the men could not comprehend the seeming lack of care that sent their top man out in the face of Merle's disclosure.

In the top of the house the moaning began, the woman in red and Jones the exiled engaged so in their ecstasy that none could sleep for fear of missing some piece of the show. But Ariél slumbered on.

THE MEN SPENT THE NEXT DAY IRRITABLE AND confused with lack of sleep, arguing over what to think about it. Corey, first thing out of his bag, reviled this Johnny: "That Jones—Johnny, Christ!—up there in that bedroom screwing the old bird while we're out here." Corey kicked at his bag, then went around the circle of bags, placed like spokes of a wheel around the hub of the dead ashes of their fireplace, blue jays screeching and cattle issuing their stentorian calls in the near distance like in imitation of the birds, sounding somehow more like donkeys in the warm morning. "Get up! All of you!" Corey kicking just hard enough to wake each man. Wes told the greaser that if he was so angry why didn't he just go out and find himself a woman of his own. Corey countered that he had, over in Anderson, and she was quite the smart little thing, but that didn't give Jones, Johnny, the right to shove it all in his face. The twins Johns had a woman in Greenville they visited alternately, separately, on horseback and posing as the same man from Texas going by the name of Sam Houston, this man's father being a direct descendant of that famed cowboy. "Hell," Wes said, in disbelief of Corey's proclamation, "all me and Tom did was talk some bullshit at a bar one night about fighting at the Alamo and that was that." Corey raged on; but most shrugged their shoulders at Jones's act, half admiring its audacity, half annoyed at the impropriety. Corey stomped away from the smoldering fire into the woods. Soon enough he was back, and finally the exhaustion from the long, hard night, with a little prodding thrown in to complete the mix, was enough impetus for Seve to join up with Corey's cause. The fat cook stood, gut draped in a white apron, serving scrambled eggs from the back of the Hummer Johnny'd picked up in El Paso before the crew tracked its way here. "The greaser is right," Seve said. "Last thing I want to hear is the sound of that goddamned copulation. While we're out here rolling around like animals on the fucking ground." Seve spit into the grass. "Sounds like the animals," he went on; being auto-bound, latched securely to the Hummer, and before, at Whitey's, to the white walls of the kitchen in the barn house, Seve didn't ride horses, didn't consort with cattle. He did an imitation of the moaning and screaming that sounded more like the throaty drone of the cattle down in the pasture. "That's it, that bastard Jones!" Corey said; suddenly Ariél was tuned into the whole thing. He said he heard no such sound, to which Seve responded with another hoot and moo, a guttural moan. "What you boys talking about?" Ariél said, just like he was a kid, eyes reflecting the stares of each and every man dumb as a genius back at himself.

"Heat, dumbo," Corey's sunglasses flashing a reflection of the morning sun and seeming to wake Ariél to the blind light of something of which he apparently had no knowledge. He let it on, anyway, and when the whole performance repeated itself that night under the bright porch light—the enraged pounding on the doorknocker, the screaming, Merle again out in the yard with the rest of the crew—Ariél slept through it like it was the run of things. The men rode with it. They watched him, this time, as the woman Nancy Miller's bright red hair glowed under the light and she banged the doorknocker. They passed jokes around about the boy's confounded innocence. "Little man, our top man, right?" Corey, again, caustic as ever, standing over the sleeping Ariél. "Never heard it in his life, can't even pick it out of the cow-sound." Nancy wailed on at the front door, and Merle whispered quick, "Watch close now," and the men turned their bodies slowly round and crouched just as the door flung open, Nancy's scream ceasing and Johnny's right arm emerging, roping her quick inside.

Ariél laughed quietly inside his dreams, for he knew the weakness of Jones, Johnny, and the inevitability of all in that dark, hot September and he felt, breathless and wild, the pluck of the next year.

WINTER CAME. NANCY WAS A FIXTURE IN THE HOUSE. After it got warm enough for the men to sleep on the hard ground in the side yard yet again, added to the sound of the braying and moaning that shot down from the top story of the house was that of ice clinking in glasses. Ariél was left to sleep and dream in peace through it all—like exceedingly randy teenage boys, the men all had their women, with no exception. Wes and Tom trotted off to Greenville in silence. Seve huffed and puffed barely audible in the bushes out toward the pasture with one of Merle's ex-wives, Merle himself laid up in the family room of the house humped over a little girl who thought his old ass was a special piece.

Every evening after test runs for the coming drive, supply runs in the Hummer to Anderson, and whatever other of the day's activities, Ariél spurred his horse and rode off toward Greenville in pursuit, the men thought, of Tom and Wes or some other diversionary moment. Ariél would never truly get his, they thought, though the top hand never spoke of what he did, seemed neither smarter nor particularly happy for the time away from his work. Deep lines set in his forehead and he rode on out.

One night over beers at Harry's, Ariél caught an obscure flick, one he'd not seen prior, in grainy black-and-white. The violent thing starred two unknowns, man and woman, cowboy and whore, who banged each other silly and, in the end, each shot the other dead over their last meal before the cowboy was to set off on a journey.

The night before Ariél and the rest of Jones's men were to set off themselves on a trail north over interstate highways and country roads, Ariél still sat idly by. Wes and Tom duked it out in front of the house over the girl in Greenville; they stood by the porch in the faint light at the edge of the motion sensor's range, both braced in boxing poses, reflections of each other, heavy-metal hair swinging around their shoulders as they traded punches to the chest. Johnny Jones, drunk, flung the door wide into the blaze of the outer light and screamed for them to cut the shit out. The light blew out promptly afterward with a spray of glass at Jones's feet, leaving his swaying form backlit in the frame of the door and flanked by the silhouette of Miss Nancy's fine, thin hair undone, the left half of her nightgown fluttering with the influx of hot night air. Jones's mouth fell open, reminding the twins in a near mumble: "Much shit to get done. Tomorrow." He disappeared inside; the twins punched on until they were both so exhausted neither could even speak to answer Ariél when he asked them if he should send word to her, for he was heading out for the night. It was already midnight, and Wesley and Thomas Johns merely looked up from their bags briefly, raising their heads, nodding, then letting them drop as if weighted.

Ariél rode, bouncing east along the freeway without a thought of the boys now behind him. Harry the proprietor awaited, and Lula May, Harry's daughter, was forever mindful of Ariél's visits. Tonight, Ariél sat directly across from the widescreen mounted into the wall. Harry shuffled over with a bottle of beer for the young man. "How is it, this evening?" he intoned, his deep, halting drawl sending a lightning pang of regret through the cowboy's bones as he settled into his seat. "OK," Ariél said, "just OK." The night was old. Lula May fluttered her eyelashes from her customary spot at the end of the bar. One hour and the place closed up for good to him; he did not tell kindly Harry, but the daughter: after four beers in quick succession and her continual inching, skipping seat by seat down the bar until she sat at Ariél's side, the caresses of her eyes sliding along the side of his head and down to the chaps he wore, he did what he'd done now seemingly forever and tried his best not to look the old man in the eye as he and Lula May rose and, arm in arm, without ceremony, disappeared behind the life-size cardboard cutout of William Perry, the former Clemson defensive tackle, through a little brown door and into the girl's room. After she'd slipped through, Ariél followed into the light of a single antique lamp, the translucent leaves of its shade casting a low glow on the wooden floor, the rickety, wood-framed, single bed where she made her way.

They wordlessly undressed, fucked, and lay in the low light naked and tired, and Ariél rose after a short time and said good-bye, a thing he'd never had to do before, with her or anyone else, preferring a quick payment or retreat to the embarrassment of mind thrust into an empty transaction. And when he did say it, Lula May frowned and thrust the money under her mattress, then smiling, sending him quietly back out into the now-empty bar and past the dark widescreen like he were a ghost, he felt. He rode back as quickly as he could, whipping and kicking at his horse under the swooping headlights of late-night tractors as they barreled around corners cut into the hillsides; a thunderstorm rolled in and drenched him as he flew along. He laid awake then for hours in the rain, nearly to sunup, and mulled over the day next: *rise, tired as ever but relieved at the end of the wait; eat; rope any of the cattle who'd wandered off into the woods or crept through the fence marking the line of Jones's, Johnny's, property to the west; take to the creek-river, deep in the bed, and pick any of the waterlogged beasts and drive them back up with the main herd, tired but again relieved for the cool burn in your muscles; lunch...* Finally he fell asleep by the extinguished fire. He dreamt of a limo ride to an unknown task, late as hell, cruising down a black swath of highway among a flatness, a brown, dusty Texas flatness, a girl he'd never met sitting just beside him in nothing but a tutu. He licked his lips, looked her over, an action that in the dream began to repeat itself: him looking the girl over with a hungry glint to his eyes, over and over again as if on constant and deliberate repeat through a VCR or other device. He woke, and it was morning. He rolled up and out of his bag, thought: *come midnight, load up the Hummer and cut out on the trail....*

AT BREAKFAST THE BOYS CROWDED AROUND SEVE'S cooker. Ariél spooned a hefty dose of scrambled egg onto his plate. A stiff thud emanated from the house, where he turned to see Jones emerge onto the porch carrying a large cardboard box, his hair matted up on one side near a foot above the top of his head. He sat the box down on the porch and whistled at the boys, motioning them over. No one made like they'd even noticed. "What's this?" Ariél turned to Corey and then pointed toward Jones, who disappeared into the house.

Corey scowled. "Must be them damned bells he's been talking about," he said.

Jones banged through the front doorway again with yet another box, dropped it, then called to Ariél, who moved as Johnny disappeared again.

"You'll see," Corey's voice cutting behind the top hand, then blossoming into violent laughter.

Each box was three-by-three-by-three feet of cardboard completely bare of any insignia. Johnny emerged with yet another, humping the box up onto the stack—the contents clinked and chimed. "I got about ten of these," Jones's voice came, barking from behind the tall stack. "Need you to take the Hummer, whenever y'all finish breakfast, take it and park it here and load these up in it," his face now appearing from behind the stack with a sarcastic smile spread over it.

"What's in them?" Ariél said.

"Cowbells," Jones said, and out across the yard, an egg-choked chorus of laughter rose from the seated circle of men.

Ariél's mind conjured an atypical rage as his heart sank; he glared back at the men and then to Jones. "Are you drunk, Johnny?"

"Cowbells," Jones barked. "You're the man for the job." He threw up his arms. Nancy appeared in the doorway, reaching out and grasping at the air between herself and her lover, who sniffed the wind like a dog. "Honey, come back to bed," she said. Jones turned round and smiled. Her pink nightgown swayed forever in the wind sucking into the house, her hair as godawful disheveled as Jones's, skin a ghostly white. Ariél's hand rose to his forehead to shield his eyes.

"And when you've got them loaded," Jones said, "get down with the herd, take Corey with you and string up every one of the beasts with one of these. I want them to sound, Goddamnit!" And Johnny now laughed, looped both hands up around his head like he were swatting flies. But suddenly he stilled, eyes glazed over full of the distance behind Ariél as if listening to the sound in his own mind. Ariél remembered for the moment why—the pull of this man. Johnny Jones dreamed hellfire and brimstone, insistently, like a child—*I want them to sound!*—Ariél helpless to argue for the moment. But at once the regret for his lot was great, and a plan drew itself in his mind that involved things he struggled for the gut to countenance, fear and loathing and betrayal, going on without the men. As if reading the top hand's mind, Jones gave a quick speech. Tonight, when they set out, it was for a town called Star they were moving, 20 miles up the trail over the freeway, just below the North Carolina border. When Ariél asked how in the name of John Wayne they would get the herd over the highway, Jones muttered "Cops." He had friends, he said, had it rigged all up the trail and over the mountains into Indiana. Ariél stood now admiring of his savior, employer, here, but it wouldn't last.

ALL DAY LONG ARIÉL AND COREY GOT PERSONAL with the beasts down in the valley mud by the creek, stringing each with a bell of her own. Corey kept referring to each and every one as "goddamned Sundance." The top hand wretched at the repetition, at the stink of them, at the stink of himself halfway through with the sweat soaking through his T-shirt and jeans, Corey all the while a veritable fountain of cool still dry in black leather in the direct sunlight. Ariél wretched at the sound, the clatter of bells growing with the progress made, near dusk rattling out of the little valley like 500 porch wind chimes hung to welcome a hurricane. The two cowboys rode up with the sound and were greeted by the stooped figure of Merle carrying the full weight of an orange easy chair down the front steps, pain in his eyes. Seve followed him down, laughing. "I told him I'd rig it," he said, "but no way would I carry it." The fat cook proceeded to fix the chair to the top of the Hummer. Merle climbed atop the vehicle at the last and sat, the full lot of the cowboys gawking at the old man. "I can't handle no horse, lads," he said. There were protests, repetitions, and out-and-out curses. The twins Johns turned to the house and screamed for Jones to get out here and tell his aged cousin how to pull his weight. The house lay silent in the gloom of the long dusk.

The herd would move at midnight, and as the time approached, the men loaded their belongings in saddle bags and prepared their horses for the journey, each in his own silent way expectant, anxious for a clear directive from their leader. Ariél muttered to himself over his horse, "Where is that bastard Jones?" and a voice came at his back, a half whisper pinched as if through clenched teeth, "I was wondering the same thing myself." Ariél spun to find Corey a few yards on and backing up a little at the fierce surprise in the top hand's eyes, then leaning conspiratorially forward. Corey turned his gaze slowly back to the house. "I don't know about you," he said, "but I got a mind to just ride off, maybe set up in Anderson, get married. I think he's nuts. Damn it if he pays me." The porch light flared into life, revealing Johnny Jones, one hand hanging tightly onto the front doorknob, Nancy still in her pink nightgown glowing there in the light; she planted a slow kiss on the back of his neck. "Look at the bastard," Corey said. "He's piss drunk." Jones swayed, moved to hang now to Nancy's shoulder. Corey tramped to the porch. Ariél watched Jones intently. When Nancy dared move away from the door, out from under the man's arm, his legs wobbled and knocked around like he'd fall clear over. Corey was saying something, gesticulating wildly; Johnny Jones responded only by struggling to raise his rolling head upright. He would not even be able to get on his horse.

Ariél hung back in the dark as the men lifted Johnny and tried to place him upright on the white horse he'd named Daisy one night back when he still hung around the fire with the men—he'd laughed and flung back his head, roared at the sky. Finally, the men succeeded and there he sat, tilted slightly to the left, face not unsmiling, looping his left hand in drunken circles as they all stood back, their gazes on the ground in front of them. "Goddamn you," Ariél muttered, all the way to the herd, night falling further thick and hot. Tom assumed Johnny's position at the point. Johnny wobbled along beside him. Wes still took the eastern point, Corey the western, moved up from his prescribed spot back along with the Hummer at the rear. The rest of the boys took the drags along each side, the mass of cattle stretching near a quarter mile in the night. They trundled with the beasts through the dark slowly across hills a mile and a half to the first major crossing, the point men stopping their horses 20 feet shy of the highway's barrier rail. The herd came to a clattering halt in a small depression between two hills, the great dissonant roar of bells eclipsing even the noise of the highway's traffic. Anchor, atop his horse secure in the center of the mass of cattle, Ariél released his reins and clapped his hands to his ears against the sound. "Goddamn you," he muttered, the rattle dying down to a low murmurous clinking as the beasts finally came to full rest. Ariél shone his flashlight along their fuzzy backs, some slick with sweat in the humid night. His own arms glistened. He watched a tractor swoop over the west hill, its headlights revealing the gently sloping precipice of the hill by degrees. A great diesel roar pierced his ears, the full blare of the headlights dawning over the herd, and like in a wave the bleats of bells washed over the beasts with the light, beginning in the rear, the outrageous din steadily rising, shooting up through the middle of the herd and now the truck's lights hitting Ariél full, the cowboy's hands moving to the sides of his head again. "Goddamn you, Jones," he said, as if that was all he could think, keeping his hands clasped firmly to either side of his head against the sound. He recalled that windy night in Bovin: the man told him his dreams of hellfire and brimstone, of his would-be comrades in arms, a people with a little less-removed tradition of driving herds north, south, west, and even sometimes east before the railroad cars came and fully shifted the paradigm. Ariél dreamt hellfire himself, dreamt with Johnny a barge stacked high with empty beer cans and whiskey bottles and the liquid once in all of the millions of them filtered through liver and kidney and flushed out through a machine gun ready to burst into flames or shoot down planes, trucks. Another diesel tractor swooped in from the west and set the beasts to clattering. When it disappeared to the east, the top hand caught the vestige of a different sound cutting through the din—someone yelled his name up front. He holstered his flashlight. A quick whistle rose from the black fog up by the highway, fell off. "Ariél!" Wes called. He answered with a whistle of his own, pulled his horse right with a quick tug, wincing at the pain in his hands, and slowly trundled toward the origin of the sound. At the edge of the herd, he spurred his horse and galloped up the east hill, turning left now, north, looking down on the mass below him, the clanging of bells reduced this far up to the sound of a kid with a play toy, the muffled scratch of an old television heard through inch-thick walls. "Ariél!" came the call again. He pushed the horse forward, Wes still invisible, the front of the herd evident only in the glint of moonlight on sweaty backs, down below. As he descended to the point, flashlight lit on the little group there, the thick stench of the herd caught in his nostrils. He spat. Wes's eyes popped with fright; Corey and Tom stood with him. "What do we do?" Wes said, left eye twitching. "What in hell do we do?" he repeated. Daisy the white horse stood, minus Johnny, over by the highway rail, her head down and munching on weeds. "Did he fall off?" Ariél said. Wes motioned to Daisy. Ariél caught her in his flashlight's beam; Johnny was there, a dark form slumped down over the horse's neck.

"He fucking passed!" Corey spat, jumping from his horse and running over to the placid pair of horse and man by the highway. He gripped the lifeless flab of Johnny's cheeks in each hand, then propped the man's chin on a fist and slapped three times in succession. After the third swat, Ariél kicked his horse forward, swung her rear around and in that violent turning pinned Corey between the animals. Corey yelped. A tendril of drool escaped from the corner of Jones's mouth and rolled over onto Corey's hatless pompadour.

"Now," said Ariél, pulling his horse away. "Will you stop?"

Corey fell to his hands and knees, panting, shaking the spit out of his hair. "Jesus!" he wheezed. Ariél brandished the whip he'd tied to his saddle horn, waved it in front of the greaser. And Corey laughed. Already the police sirens wailed, the noise rising and topping the east and west hills and seeming to converge dissonantly in the space above the small circle of cowboys. Ariél snaked the whip just over the top of the greaser's pompadour, the tail of the whip grabbing a lock and pulling it straight into the air. Wes and Tom winced at the menace in the act. "You coming with me?" Corey said, still laughing despite it all. Then he bounced backward, hopped into the left stirrup and flung his right leg over his horse, kicking her hard in the same motion. "I'll remind you, you don't own that horse," Ariél said, "and no, I'm not coming with you." Corey kicked her into a gallop up the western rise, where he disappeared.

"We can just leave these bastards here," Ariél addressed the twins, motioning back to the herd, "or we can take them forward." He raised a fist back toward the road, shaking it into the darkness. Tom then told how Johnny'd gone on and on about Nancy like a teenage boy, kept pulling from a flask he'd stowed in a saddle bag until it just got the best of him. "I think he's been drunk all day," Tom said. Ariél fished the flask from Johnny's bag and pulled himself, grateful for the whiskey sting in his throat. And now the cops were nearly in position; the rotating blue of the lights flashed behind the blackness of both east and west hills. Light splashed into the valley. "Let's take them across," Ariél said.

Tom told him it was half-past, making reference to 1AM, the cops early by a quarter hour, no use waiting. It was too late anyway to call off the boys on the edges, who would be pushing forward presently—the cops' arrival was their cue. "Watch this," Ariél declared, then thinking to himself the punch line: famous last words. He raised the whip once more, flicked his wrist in Johnny's direction and took a chunk of skin near an inch in diameter from the bare meat of the drunk's triceps. The arm swayed a little, hung there down over the front left shoulder of that brilliant white horse. Ariél laughed; Tom and Wes looked on in mild wonder as blood began to trickle down the man's arm.

Ariél popped him again, the crack of the whip sounding above the burgeoning racket of bells now at their backs, the nearer the sirens came, the beasts responding to an excess of sound other than their own, it seemed. "He's useless. Dogshit," Ariél said. One last tractor beat the police lights over the west hill and blew by, raising an uproarious clatter. The cowboys back along the drags atop the east and west hills started their whooping, some belting screams and others curt whistles that brought the bell-clatter and moaning to a crescendo from the rear of the herd. Ariél could hear Seve's foot on the Hummer's gas a quarter-mile back, imagined the lanky Merle in the big easy chair swiveling slowly to Seve's steering. The din rose as the rear of the herd pushed forward, so much so that Ariél had to yell his instructions to Wes to take Johnny to the back: "Put Merle on my horse and send him up along the drags.

Tom, take Corey's front flank up the west hill." Ariél jumped from his horse and traded saddle bags with Daisy. Wes and Tom jumped down and helped him lift the man's dead weight from the saddle and drape the drunk across the neck of Wes's horse. The twins heaved while Ariél mounted the white mare, took another pull from Johnny's flask and brandished the whip. The police cruisers stood monolithic each at the precipice of the surrounding hills, sirens blazing. "Go Wes, now, not much time." The front line of cattle had trundled ever forward at the racket raised by the cowboys behind them. Wes galloped up the east hill and disappeared into the darkness. "Let's take the beasts across," Ariél said.

"Do you know where we're headed?" Tom turned his horse, swung her around quickly, her legs bobbing, knees bending, head wagging back and forth in limbo before gallop.

"I don't imagine it matters," Ariél nearly whispered the words, faced the road, whip in hand, outrageously steely squint to his eyes, lips pursed, then parted just to a thin black line and sucking in air: Watch this, he wanted to say, again, like the stupid child of some dumb hick, standing face full over the rim of an empty beer bottle, M-80 firecracker in his right hand, burning match in the other. "Watch this," the child says, turning wide-eyed and grinning to his friends—the M-80 blows his hand clear off. He has to spend the rest of his school days learning to write with his left, dies hard after being beaten horribly on school grounds by the bullies who made fun of him.

"Famous last words," Ariél said, or maybe he didn't even say it, simply thought it, thought the punch line, thought too that that wasn't even the punch line, but rather the setup. *Watch this shit* was the punch line. *Redneck's last words?*—delivered by a half-bald stooge of a stand-up artist on late-night TV with wide eyes and a silly, expectant look on his face, arms outstretched. *Watch this shit Goddamnit!* to the tune of roaring laughter and applause.

Tom gave the top hand a frightful look, turned his horse and galloped up the west hill to assume the front flank. Ariél raised his whip, cracked it on Daisy's tail and whooped his own high-rebel yell as she jumped hard over the highway rail, followed by the herd like sheep to a shepherd. Ariél galloped across the highway's asphalt in the din. He pulled hard on the reins before reaching the other side, raising Daisy up on her rear legs. She gleamed pristinely white in the rotary incandescence of the police lights. He produced a chrome cap pistol from his bag, set Daisy down and spurred her onward, gun in the air, popping incessantly.

ARIÉL LED THE TROOP IN ZIGZAGS THROUGH THE forest on the other side, the herd breaking up almost immediately, loud and dirty chaos the tune, cattle split in two or otherwise flattened by rigs when the policemen fled the scene in rabid panic, realizing the enterprise was far out of control and refusing any culpability for their part in it—blood spewed from thick veins; hot spit flew. The poor bastard cows had a time keeping up with the galloping of the point man, Ariél, who left the herd behind in a matter of minutes. The lot of the men converged in the dawn back where they had begun, under the watch of a drunk still passed out and being fanned and fawned over by his old dirty lady. For months afterward justices of the peace were following up, care of requests filed by Johnny Jones, on reports of burly steer corralled in the backyards of tall, double-jointed men who chewed tobacco on cinderblock steps to flimsy trailers west of Greenville, only in SC, but Ariél was not among them. The short Chicano lived out his days at Harry's under the soft light of Miss Lula May's lamp, in the little bedroom, and emerged nights, tended bar for aging Harry. If Jones had had the entrepreneurial spirit to seek him out, maybe he'd have found the man, just under his nose as he was. But he hadn't. The herd now barely half its original size, Jones corralled the men themselves for another try the next year, or the next next, forgoing the need of a replacement for Ariél for the greaser Corey, who returned upon hearing of the failure. Men could only wonder.

TO SUBMIT TO OUR ENEMIES NOW, WOULD BE MORE INFAMOUS THAN IT WOULD HAVE BEEN IN THE BEGINNING. IT WOULD BE COWARDLY YIELDING TO POWER WHAT WAS DENIED UPON PRINCIPLE. IT WOULD BE TO YIELD THE CHERISHED RIGHT OF SELF-GOVERNMENT, AND TO ACKNOWLEDGE OURSELVES WRONG IN THE ASSERTION OF IT; TO BRAND THE NAMES OF OUR SLAUGHTERED COMPANIONS AS TRAITORS; TO FORFEIT THE GLORY ALREADY WON; TO LOSE THE FRUITS OF ALL THE SACRIFICES MADE AND THE PRIVATIONS ENDURED; TO GIVE UP INDEPENDENCE NEARLY GAINED, AND BRING CERTAIN RUIN, DISGRACE AND ETERNAL SLAVERY UPON OUR COUNTRY. THEREFORE, UNSUBDUED BY PAST REVERSES, AND UNAWED BY FUTURE DANGERS, WE DECLARE OUR DETERMINATION TO BATTLE TO THE END, AND NOT TO LAY DOWN OUR ARMS UNTIL INDEPENDENCE IS SECURED. IS LIFE SO DEAR, OR PEACE SO SWEET, AS TO BE PURCHASED AT THE PRICE OF CHAINS AND SLAVERY? FORBID IT HEAVEN!

Resolution 4, adopted by McGowan's Brigade,
South Carolina Volunteers, 1865

FOR ONE, I FOUND OUT MY BROTHER WAS DEAD IN January of the next year. Albert called and gave me the news. Bobby Jones had served his time for killing our mother—a thing near ten years gone and, though it was frankly impossible, almost forgotten—and within a week he was taken down by pneumonia, of all things. "I was having a damn time of it," Albert said, "keeping him still in that room, as it were. Though he never did seem to want to leave it in the accepted fashion. And I mean through the goddamned doorway." My brother is, well, was, crazy as a rat: that's what I told Albert. "Well hell I know that. Believe me, Bill, I know it..." Albert said he found the boy after only the second night of his freedom on the porch with a bottle of whiskey Albert had given him, being a believer in its healing power, much like myself. Unfortunately for crazy Bobby it was the dead of winter and a particularly cold night. My brother had gone through the window in his little room in Albert's house and ended up on the porch. His bare feet were propped up on the front rail where Albert normally laid his own; he sat conked out there asleep and in a shivering fever in the early dawn light when Albert found him. Albert said he brought the crazy son of a bitch back in dry as a sheet and drunk, and it was only to get worse from there.

Secondly, Artichoke Heart was back after a brief and failed attempt at South Carolina life, which he could not hack but for a short six months. His brothers, the rest of his band, said they needed to be there, their old mother and the rest of their ancestors were buried there, and they sucked up the region like addicts, wanted to pick it all up there, though I'd always known that without A.H. and his bravura and trumpet-blast bombast, his full vinyl jumpsuit, they wouldn't last long. A.H. was back in Chicago, yes, and I couldn't have been happier, in spite of the cold. He'd taken a job at the Two-Way, of all places, to supplement the dwindling savings from his large days. I called him when I heard about Bobby and gave him the news. He knew the old story, if he couldn't comprehend the why. We met up at Johnny's Grill and sat in the sun by the window, looking out into the traffic circling monotonously about the square. A.H. wore his mirrored shades; I wore mine. His tiara perched in full crimson glory atop the crown of his head.

"Why?" he asked. "I wonder, though maybe I do get it." A.H. didn't look away from the square. Neither did I. We stared through our mirrors into the cars and the eagle-topped monument staring, in turn, straight back at us. Its monolithic import never quite penetrated our cold eyes to make an impression on the blockhead brains behind them this cold Saturday afternoon. A.H. waited for the explanation. My insides brewed with apprehension, knowing he waited. He stirred his coffee. I brought a piece of toast I'd paid for with one of my last dollars into my mouth and chewed.

Then, I began, "Whenever anyone asks me why he killed her, I always do recall a little battle my father had with a cop over his gun. I was 16, out on a weekend night with a girl named Molly. Bobby sat at a babysitter's, even at 13; Pop never let him do so much on account of his general horniness, hyperactivity, and inattention. The boy was a solid part of the Ritalin-fed alliance of teenage psychos then ravaging the town's landscape."

"The newest of the new white Souths," A.H. said, which I didn't quite want to understand, but that's all right. I doubt he fully understood it himself.

"Bobby was always a bit of a weird kid—wild and reckless, like his father. When he was in grammar school, before the onset of the wonder pill, fistfights seemed to sort of follow him around. But he was also overly thoughtful like his mother. Talking to Bobby was a little maddening. It was like he refused to relinquish control of the conversation, or rather to even participate in it at all." I stared into the sun-bleached square and remembered my last conversation with the boy, which I related to A.H. It went something like this:

Hey Bobby.
Billy.
How is it?
You said no one deserves it.
How's everything?
It's all right, I guess.
Seeing much of Albert?

You said no one deserves to die, I remember. And Bobby said not even Hitler?

That's right, I did say that and I fucking meant it.

If Hitler were alive and over Germany we might just all have a little more fun and less Jews. Mr. Albert said that.

Did he?

The guy in the cell next to me is a Jew. He's a dirty fucker too.

"...this is prison stuff, of course. I used to try to call him quite often, though I was only occasionally allowed to actually engage in this sort of stuff. There were regulations I never totally understood. He was more than a little crazy, though, even before the joint. By his first year of high school he was wildly popular for his nut talk. Folks thought it was just him putting on a show of weirdness, right? After he went to prison, it got worse. Everything about his character exploded, and all his little tics compounded into grotesquery."

When asked why Bobby took my (actually my buddy Eric's) gun and topped my mother, I am forever really at a loss to explain it. I told A.H. this again and he said he figured that was just me afraid of it or something. "I think I understand the compulsion to kill, but you haven't told me the story yet," he said.

I ignored him, mostly, though it wasn't hard to imagine A.H. pulling the plug on somebody. His hard brown eyes, the sunken lines in his face that came vertically down from under his eyes clear to the corners of his mouth, like it'd spent a lifetime coiled up in a rage at something or other; it'd make perfect sense for him to be standing with a baseball bat at an angle to his hip over the bashed-in head of some senseless prick.

"By his first year of high school, Bobby was in with the smart and senseless, drugged-out crew. But that particular night he'd been at a babysitter's. Pop picked him up, as my mother was up at Lake Junaluska in North Carolina at some church-related gathering. Pop was drunk and smelled it, I'm sure. A cop pulled him over and the officer didn't recognize who he was. If he had, of course, Johnny Jones being who Johnny Jones was, the bastard, that cop would likely have let the matter alone. But Johnny Jones's license, even, his own name, meant nothing to this man, and he raised Pop out of the car to the side of the road and had him walk the line and stand on one foot while counting out one to ten Mississippi and all. In those days Pop carried a pistol around with him. Bobby was the only other person in the car, and he was drooling all over himself, sniveling with a case of the flu in the passenger seat. He'd been asleep when it began so was completely incapacitated, groggy, for the first few minutes of the affair. Though by the time the cop finished up with humiliating half-drunk Johnny Jones, Bobby had perked up enough to recognize what was up and to do what was needed for his father. Pop had miraculously 'passed' the sobriety tests, but the cop he wasn't satisfied, so he commenced searching the car. Johnny had lied, of course, about their being no firearms in the car. Essentially, he'd denied it, that question set characteristically up against the one about drugs. 'Got any illegal substances, firearms, weapons of any kind,' barked systematically, part of the unceasing litany of demands made automatically by the American Gestapo. Of course he didn't mean anything by it, so Johnny Jones might be said to have 'failed to remember,' if you like, that his own pistol lay snug under the passenger seat.

"At the time, South Carolina's laws prohibited 'concealed' firearms, meaning that if you had a piece you better have it clear up in a gun rack or something. He'd forgotten about it. My father told me this and I believed it, believe it or not. Thing is, when the cop gave his obligatory 'Well, then you won't mind me—' and he searched the car, found the piece, and this is the hinge of the whole event, I'm saying, the thing that matters, that holds it all together.

"When the cop found the pistol, Bobby took the fall."

A.H. turned toward me. We stared into each other's reflections for a length of time uncertain as the seconds dragged out to the erratic ticks that resounded from the cooler behind the counter, where Dean stood wiping said cooler's metallic top clear of the grease that coats everything in the place. "He took the fall," A.H. said.

"That's right," I said. "He somehow managed to convince the cop, sniveling with that flu all the while, that Johnny didn't know nothing about the gun. 'I put it in here,' Bobby said. 'It's his, but I put it in here. He didn't know nothing about it. I wanted to show it to my friends.' For which Bobby received quite a lecture from the stone-faced cop, but for him it was better than watching Pop go down on this night. My mother told me all about it the next day when she got home, as it left her feeling quite miffed and even maybe outraged, I'd say, at Mr. Johnny Jones for letting Bobby go on like that—but she was also a little jealous. Bobby never moved toward her like that, skulked around her silently and just took what she handed to him on the way out the door: lunch in a brown paper bag, one of his many medications, notes—she communicated mostly with the boy in notes handed to him when he left into the sunny Carolina afternoon or to school, though he sat out any number of days any given week. In the end, Bobby would do anything for Pop, attributing a quality of greatness to him I'd done my unsuccessful best to distill. And so if I blame anyone for the death of my mother, it is my father. That's it, I've said it, though he didn't necessarily want the deed done in any kind of literal way. He wanted rid of her, I'm sure, though hadn't the kind of exacting sense of his own desires in this case to put forth a direct plan, one he'd be culpable for. He and Bobby talked to each other sometimes like they were old chums. Bobby was too young to deal with it, took the old man's complaints about mother as a mandate, I think. That leaves me, myself, alone to pick up the pieces, because, as I say, my father may not have wanted it done, but when it was done and my mother dead in the ground and my little brother in jail, he took all of his money and fled the town. The last time I talked to him was the day I left the state myself. I happened to run into him at a gas station outside of Blacksburg on my way out. We barely even said a thing to each other. I hear only scant word from Albert Ledbetter, who's an old pal of my father's and my main source of information about the town and the man."

I went on and explained to A.H. the Great Listener the whole conundrum, as I saw it, of the sonless father Albert who basically took to Bobby as one would his own flesh and blood. A.H. went on staring into the ice and snow and traffic around the square. The cold penetrated everything, the snow caking onto the stone leaves up around the figure of the Nazi eagle atop the monument. A.H. was back. "How do we stand this cold?" I asked him. I turned my mirrored aviators left, to him, to discover that his mirrored gaze was no longer fixed out of the window, that here he was looking at me looking now at him. "Why didn't you bring some of that damn warm weather back up here with you?" I said.

He didn't reply to this either, only smiled and then looked away when I caught my own goofy, smiling face again in the mirrors of his shades, and we limped up from our stools and burst into the afternoon, rugged and brilliant and with our hands shoved into our pockets, feet cracking along the icy sidewalk back south down Milwaukee Avenue toward his home, where he decamped, saying, "It's times like these one needs a drink," and me saying I'd see him later at the bar, the Two-Way, yes? He'd be working this evening.

Then I must have walked for hours down Milwaukee in the cold, sunny afternoon, all the way downtown, a distance of miles, certainly, past bodegas and dollar stores and the consignment shops in Wicker Park and on down through the industrial sector by the chocolate factory, whose stench is inescapable, unbearable; even in the cold it hangs thickly in the air and sticks to the skin of your upper lip. I ended my sojourn at nightfall over the wreckage of a derailment on the Amtrak commuter tracks under the Randolph Street bridge by the river. How they would get the behemoth of a train out of there I could not comprehend. Its silvery top was pocked here and there with ice from the intermittent snows we'd had these past days. It was a monstrous wreck, bringing to mind nothing other than itself. It appeared workers had been digging the railcars out, one by one, from the twisted track and surrounding fill. The last of the three I could see was lined with big mounds of earth near high as the compartments themselves: the beginning, I guessed.

I wasn't at all sure how I would get home from here: there were buses, trains, cabs, but I didn't have the cash really to spare for any of them. The check from my phone-pumping job was due on Tuesday. The light had passed now entirely from the sky. The wind whipped up coming in west off the lake. I'd forgotten my gloves. Such was the way. I thought of my stupid brother damn near frozen to death on crazy Albert's porch with a bottle. I wanted to drink, still had time before I told A.H. I'd meet him, so I walked farther into the Loop with my hands deep in the pockets now of my jeans, closer to my flesh, and passed under the tracks at Wells and into the front of the Fermata, hoping Kate would spot me a few. I hadn't seen her since Independence Day, and though I didn't have much desire to face the certain discomfort of this meeting, considering our last, barely remembered whirl, the need to get drunk outweighed any reservation. I passed the suit-clad doormen, walked under the cheap crystal chandelier lighting up this side of the lobby suddenly conscious of my windblown hair, my jeans, my smelly thrift-store leather coat—this room was immaculate. I popped into the bar area through the wooden swinging doors and stopped dead in my tracks; the place was almost completely dark and silent, an ambience I couldn't explain. I peered into the darkness, my eyes eventually adjusting to the point lighting that illuminated the ceiling and every wall. "Wow," I muttered. The place had had a total makeover. I took a halting step forward before the bartender, presumably—who I still could not make out back there in the dark haze—barked "Can I help you?" like she were a McDonald's clerk or a cop.

I squinted through the low light. Was it Kate? I asked, hearing something vaguely familiar in that brogue. "Excuse me?" she said, again as a cop or a pissed trailer-park queen.

"I'm looking for Kate?" I said, now just able to make the woman out.

Then, softer, "Oh," she said, the word floating out of and then back into her mouth, muffled by what I imagined to be her hands. I could hear her feet scuttling back and then out of range. "Hello?" I said, and began to inch forward, hands in front of me, level with my stomach, until they grabbed the edge of the bar. I opened my eyes and realized they'd been closed—the bar was lit by the dim points set into the walls, but the coverage was great, colossal and bright compared to the blackness behind my eyelids. A sick fear surged through my stomach as I plopped down on the nearest stool.

"Excuse me?" came a voice, less angered than the one before. I looked up and a woman stood staring at me from the doorway to the back employees' area. "You're looking for Kate Wolfe?"

This woman was beautiful: dark brown hair cut short and falling naturally around her eyebrows, her ears, the back of her neck. Blue eyes keen and somehow sad, too. My fear passed almost instantly. "Yes, I haven't seen her in quite a time," I said, smiling now at this wonderful apparition. She half-smiled back, but was obviously thinking hard behind her eyes.

"Kate is dead," she said, and her tears belied the apparent truth of the statement. The woman burst into a fit and then her friend, a girl I remembered from the days I frequented the place—and whom I took to be the crying lady's gruff counterpart—rushed from the back and put her arms around her coworker's shoulders, giving me an utterly helpless look, not mad or even the least bit perturbed. I stood from my stool.

"It's OK," I said. "I didn't know. I was just in the area and—" my short speech broken here by the pretty woman's wailing; through the intelligible portions I gathered that my friend the Virginian Kate met her demise by way of a mugger with a pistol, just a block away from the Fermata's front doors, two weeks prior, and the woman continued to cry. I backed away from the bar slowly, muttering damn near incoherently absurd apologies and murmurs of empathy, that I didn't know, had no idea, couldn't possibly have and that I was sorry, so sorry, before suddenly tripping up on a round table or high chair which sent me reeling back on my heels. I woke on the floor with a pillow under my head, staring straight into the series of lights on the ceiling; they were arranged in a pentagram. The pretty woman's tear-streaked, made-up face hung maybe a foot above my own. "Hell," I said, that sick, inexplicable fear knotting in my stomach; I stood up quick, bumping the pretty lady a little on my way. She wobbled a bit coming to her feet, as did I, which brought another half smile to her face. But I couldn't think of a thing to say. Kate, gone. Bobby. Each in their own disgusting manner. I thought about my mother while I stared at the woman and wanted to lay down on the carpeted floor of the place with her and whisper into her ear while she cried it out herself and I cried some more and maybe we'd screw each other silly, yes. But I must have gotten a sadistic gleam in my eye, for the smile on her face disappeared, and her thin lips flattened into a line like she was scared or pissed or both. She ran into the back and left me there alone in the dim light.

I froze near to death on the way home, in the dark. It began to snow about 30 minutes into the journey, and by the time I'd reached the Two-Way I needed a good thawing out. I sat dripping at the bar when A.H. strolled in for his shift. He assumed his position behind the two taps. Before the night was over and I got completely shitfaced, he told me an insane story about having once had to kill an old white alderman somewhere on the city's south side, a favor to none other than Nova Capone, a good-time hipster gangster from South America or someplace who was dead, last I heard. I didn't believe a fucking word of it at the time, content to rage at the audacity of the telling—here I am and A.H. well knows my brother is newly dead, I've just told him of my friend Kate, and my goddamned mother and all…

I just shook my head and wanted to say, "We'll be all right, right? I mean we're not fucking nuts or anything?" but I didn't say a word. He dropped another beer in front of me. I gazed through the drunken haze to his big black face and that damn tiara on his head and I thought that if there weren't success or comfort in my bones or this place, at least there was the typical. People die and fall apart, and the rest of us roll along, drunk and divine to the last.

ALL OF WHICH—THE DRUNKEN THINKING, THE approach of the dead—brought on the last of my preoccupations, that which would keep me for a time from engaging any sort of worthy enemy, much less the swashbuckling warrior president the Texan was becoming. After that mad night at the Two-Way I joined the stars and planets and heaven-sent panels of experts who seemed to make a great cohort designed to rid me of purpose—I joined them in reacting to the deadly chaos around me by clinging to a noble consistency. Sofie was not coming back. Elsa, who'd left with much more than just the clean apartment, timely rent check, neat bookshelf, etc, continued to occupy my daydreams. One particularly persistent vision had her appearing at my doorstep, purple vinyl-covered suitcase in tow.

A.H. continued to insist that the women were only cogs in some sort of eternal-return vortex I was all caught up in, a fractured and pathetically outmoded TV-rerun pastiche of sorts. Though didn't Nietzsche place a positive moral value on that norm? Neither could I remember nor really give a shit, truthfully, as a brimming confidence in the idea had instituted itself in my head and heart, and a man named E.J. Pinkerton, a bluesman with the head of a turkey, a harmonica, and no facial expression to speak of, instructed me in the dreamy early morns on many aspects of my existence, though mostly my attire. *Consistency* here was the watchword as well; I spent a year that way, the next few months of winter and on into spring and summer and fall and into winter again I wore the same hard black leather oxfords on my feet every day. I rotated around ten or so pairs of black corduroy pants picked up at a vintage-80s shop selling mostly department-store overstock: old and imperfect, yet unused, leftovers from the glory days of Sears and others like it. On my upper half, I wore the stock white Hanes tee, rotating again between a good ten or so, and on particularly cold days I substituted a thermal undershirt. I walked to the train to work with a slight swagger; I walked steadily, quickly homeward after like I'd been riding it all day. Though really I'd been eight hours in a little half cubicle lifting a phone to catch my cigarette smoke–laden breath. I'd sit at my computer at home and record everything that had happened throughout the day, careful not to upset the lonely, delicate balance I'd made. I spent what little was left of the night at the Two-Way or another wayward bar, blasting all memory of the day out of my head with booze.

When all the walking reduced the pile weave of the corduroy between my legs to the thickness of cheesecloth, when the armpits of my white shirts inevitably took on a brown-yellow color and went stiff, I'd hurtle down to the "vintage" store and the local Target, respectively, and restock. This, anyway, had been the general idea. But the clothes never decayed enough to warrant it. That next spring came, and as it was ending I received fire one woeful Wednesday yet again from old-boy Albert Ledbetter. He wanted to warn me of a trip he was making to Chicago. Actually, it couldn't be considered a warning so much as a kindly notice, for he figured somehow I'd enjoy this, a week's worth of himself and his fat friend Tope Talbert—two old men who had, just a month prior, stumbled upon a Saturday liquor delivery in the middle of town, a big behemoth of a truck idling out front of the ABC spirits shop with the back rolling door on the cargo box standing wide open, the driver nowhere to be found. Albert and Tope, both already drunk at the time, midafternoon shuffling around town in the blazing Southern sun and heat, pulled that rolling door with all the weak alcoholic strength they could muster: they whacked the lock down with a great thrum and rattle, and came away with a year and more's supply of free booze.

Or so Albert told me. Maybe he was lying.

His voice crackled through the bad connection I always get from my hometown. It's like the men and women down there live in caves, dripping peanut butter walls absorbing the sound, then spitting it back out the other side in furry fragments. "We stole the damn thing," he said, more hushed than before. "It's parked out at Tope's father's old lake house, back in the bushes and trees behind it. The house is rotted all to hell..." his voice rising and splintering again as he trailed off on a tangent about how he and Tope and my crazy father once blew the old lake house porch clear off with some dynamite they'd rigged to it from Benny James's stash—just for the hell of it—when they were kids. Benny was a black man, a rabble-rouser near my grandfather's age but more suited for my crazy father's company. Benny, however, seemed to have clearer motives for his own terrific schemes. My father and Albert did shit for shit's sake.

Albert made sure I remembered that Benny was dead of a heart attack.

"Poor Benny's dead over a couple years now," he said.

"Yes, you did tell me so," I said. He'd already said it twice.

"Did I tell you that poor bastard died?"

"Back to the story, Mr. Albert. If you would."

I heard him strike a match, blow smoke with a rush of noise. Then came whirring: "Huh?"

"The liquor truck."

Albert could string syllables together like an auctioneer when he was worked up: his voice squeezed from his peanut-butter cave a high-pitched, squeaky thing. I tucked the phone between my shoulder and ear, put my hands behind my head and leaned back, listening, settling in for the round. "Yep so we stole it," Albert said, rapid fire. "Tope wants to get out of town for-a-bit-and-cool-them-big-heels."

"You driving the truck up?" I asked him. This sounded a bit outrageous, though these two driving the stolen thing 12 hours north full of stolen liquor just for a few days' drunk among bright Chicago streets…I'd not discount the possibility for a second.

But Albert told me that, indeed, they were not: "Tope's got a goddamn-near-brand-new GMC-twenty-five-hundred…"

Thing is, I couldn't fully believe they were actually coming, or didn't want to, maybe. I may have mentioned it to A.H. at the bar later that night, even, though I don't think I accepted it. I got drunk at the Two-Way, uneventfully, and afterward weaved my way up Milwaukee Avenue, through the square, bouncing over cracks in the sidewalk. I sat down in front of my computer, the .txt file where I recorded my days. In a moment of drunken whimsy at the beginning of it, half recalling something Artichoke Heart once told me about humans and monkeys and things jotted down, I'd typed "FOR A LITERATURE OF PRISTINE AND COMPLETE STUPIDITY" at the precipice of the document and what followed was my life for the last year. I'd written near two hundred pages, all drawn up by the minutes—

> 8:03AM: wake, yet another dream fizzling in head and out of ears of E.J. Pinkerton's guttural wailing from the chicken/turkey beak deep down below a false phantom radio broadcast about a proposed O'Hare airport deal. Always an airport problem really, never a deal. Expansion, retraction, a new airport proposed for construction in a little town whose

> name has likely never before been pronounced outside of its own limits. Mayor/General/Mayor/Governor.
> 8:14: breakfast of coffee and four cigarettes smoked in quick succession on bed.
> 8:20: resolve to follow E.J.'s directive: hum forlorn songs, wear your highwater corduroys.
> 8:22: wash face; dress lower half of body first. Smoke another cigarette on bed. Dress upper half of body. Rush to train.
> 8:35: on train, note cute blonde seated next to her customarily redheaded friend, noting you, in turn, as she will. Grip chrome pole and sway as train sends you up into the light. Blush at blonde's meek, shifty-eyed glancing. Look around at stone-faced customers to see if anyone has noticed the budding erection pressing against the barrier of your corduroy. Wonder how old she is, for the zillionth time. Assume she's much, much too young. Determine, once again—act on nothing, act on nothing…

—and so on, though I made a habit of not reading over the old entries after they were put down, if only for consistency's sake, the "diary" representative of a kind of method by which I further expunged the trudge of days. Also, the entries were by nature fragmentary. That particular night I didn't record much past the previous morning's hangover cure, much like my breakfast, appropriately enough: coffee, four cigarettes. I passed out in my desk chair, woke up sometime around 4AM blinded by the gloomy blue buzz of the screen saver's swirl. I rose, stumbled over the mountains of white shirts and corduroys that covered my floor, flinging myself at last onto my twin bed. I dreamt again of my turkey-headed bluesman; this time he was the incarnation of photos I'd seen of my father's dead friend Benny, with a harelip (or -beak, rather) and all. Benny/E.J. strummed an old banjo this time cloaked in darkness but for his blank, ghoulish face. And he had nothing for me. "What will you tell me, sir? Please," I pleaded with him. He just kept playing.

Thursday rolled by without incident. From the morning's preponderant haze of recollection I'd nearly forgotten about everything. I didn't even make it out to the Two-Way that night. I resumed my precarious routine—typed for an hour after a quick dinner and sprawled atop the pile of clothes on my floor in front of TV sitcom reruns, thinking, quite amazed, to myself how my life—all of it, everything—had happened.

THE ALBERT R. PARSONS CENTER—WHICH HOUSED, among other entities, my employer, the Illinois Department of Waste Management—sits at the junction of every rapid-transit line in the city apart from one. Folks from all over—the bombed-out west side, froufrou near north, stodgy southwest—meet in the panoptic interior, among the 20-plus floors splayed three-fourths of the way around an open center which falls to a lower atrium. A food court sends its vague stink wafting upward into state offices. The German who designed the building has got to be one of the most sinister jokesters in history. The Parsons Center can boast the highest suicide-attempt rate of all of Chicago's buildings. On the top floor, a viewing area with only a four-foot-high guardrail gives visitors and workers alike a full-on view all the way down to the circular atrium on the ground floor—a mandala-like design built into the tile 20 stories down that, to the suicidal among us, could only look like a target to be hit for the full spectacle. The self-anointed victim catches the momentarily waking eyes of each floor's sleepy desk drones as he/she falls in his/her brief final moment of notoriety on this earth, a swan dive to a splat dead center of that design, to the tune, then, after the magnificent whack, of the oohing and ahhing of thousands of the surrounding city's workers at peace, spooning their lunches in the lower food court. I'd never actually witnessed this, though it had happened at least four times in the couple years I'd worked there. I always seemed to miss it by seconds, catching only the resulting phalanx of police and medics.

Lately, at the center of the mandala design, the city had rested one of its "Cows on Parade," a concrete, life-size cow that was part of a citywide public-art project, with artists commissioned to decorate one of the beasts however they liked. The Parsons Center cow was the obligatory Irish cow, painted with four-leaf clovers, and was mostly, simply, green.

My desk sat very near the inner walkway on our floor, facing out into the open center next to others who worked the switchboards of different departments. Friday, sitting high in my chair, I commanded a view over the top of my computer's monitor of the visitor viewing area on the top floor—across the open-air expanse, up two floors and to the left of the twinkling glass elevators that rose up the center of the three-quarter panopticon like a surveillance tower. The phone rang constantly, all morning long. I answered, "Waste Management, this is…," transferred, answered, transferred. I never ate breakfast. Usually this wasn't a problem, but by lunchtime today a small headache I'd had when I woke up, fed by the ringing phone and otherwise starved of any sustenance, had bloomed into an entirely new state of pain.

Before lunch, I made a call to check my home answering machine; a crushing reminder lay in wait. Albert's voice whined over the line from someplace in Tennessee, he said. "Just a friendly reminding. We'll be there come tomorrow morning, nine-in-the-A-M-or-such, I'd say." I could hear Tope grunting in the background. "Oh yeah," Albert went on. "Tope here wants to know if you've got-a-cot-or-something for him to sleep on." I hung up the phone, stared for a moment at my computer monitor and breathed. Slowly. Preparing mentally to meet the men tomorrow and make sure they'd at least reconsider staying with me. The pain boomed at the back of my head. I had no ideas, for now, other than maybe dirtying up my place a little more, being careful to point out how godawfully small it was, that someone would be sleeping in the goddamned closet, take it all. It could work; I imagined Albert to be something of a picky, crotchety bastard, anyhow.

And then I looked up, just above the top of the monitor and out across the center emptiness. At the precipice of the elevators, in the visitor viewing area, stood a man wearing incongruously what looked like a black cape or trench coat. He was sweating, bent at the waist and leaned over the edge of the guardrail, staring into the abyss below. His hair was long, but the top of his head was mostly bald. Rapt, I watched him stand straight and back away, disappearing into the offices or elsewhere. I wanted to see one jump, I really did—in spite of the physical horror the aftermath surely would be, a man so very starved for attention was compelling as an idea, at least. My eyes fixed there for a full two minutes after he'd disappeared.

"Billy Goddamnit! Get a haircut, please—" I spun around in my chair to find my boss, whom I hadn't seen in over a month, had to be, standing at the edge of my cubicle shaking his head back and forth in disapproval.

“Well sir,” I said, mock-fluffing the hair around my ears with both hands like a woman. Normally the guy was good for a laugh.

“Cut that shit out,” he said, then proceeded to debunk my entire method by complaining about my woefully inappropriate attire. Not like it was the first time, though. “This is an office,” he said, then went on about how this call center was a grouping of professionals and not what it may have appeared, to me, to be, which was in truth a group of mostly middle-aged single Hispanic women with nothing much better to be doing with their time—and me. He waved his hand as if to indicate myself and cubicle. “And clean this place up, for Jesus sake.” Old newspapers coated the floor and all available desk space. Maybe he had a point. And to cap it, he said, “I’ll need you to stay two hours late today. Mona’s sick, won’t be coming in.” My head felt like it would explode backward into my computer screen, blood and brains sprayed in an arc over the outer walk’s railing, down to the cow in the food court below. My face flushed. I muttered through clenched teeth the first thing that came to mind. “You goddamned dwarf turd—” barely audible, I guess, but loud enough, for my boss’s face lit up and his fist came slamming onto the top of a pile of newspapers on my desk. The resulting thud, puny compared to the fury with which that fist was brought down, was so very pathetic that I laughed. Then came the proverbial “That’s it. You’re fired.”

I could not quit laughing, despite the grief the whole thing would cause me in the weeks to come. I turned in my chair, laughing, back to my computer as he huffed off through the maze of cubicles. I was still laughing near a full minute later when I looked up to the visitor viewing area and saw the caped man now perched at full height atop the guardrail, his knees wobbling and the rest of his body swaying precariously. He stood for a few moments more, gaining his balance, willful before the plunge. He closed his eyes. His chest bulged as he took a deep breath like to buoy himself up. His legs locked, knees slightly bent and poised. He smiled, happy like nothing I’d seen for some time. And, a half second before three security guards, with their hands beckoning at his back, could get to him, he further bent his knees, arms flung wide from his sides, and sprung into the air.

A LITTLE WOBBLY-KNEED MYSELF, NOT TEN MINUTES later, I hobbled through the maze of cubicles, shiny nameplate from my cubicle in hand—WILLIAM HARMONY JONES, CALL CENTER. I would steal my archenemy Dewey Dilbert's own (DEWEY DILBERT, PARSONS CENTER SURVEILLANCE) for the last time. I would stuff it in my bag and wave good-bye to months of his bespectacled insinuations, my own: over the months he'd been here, I'd occasionally intercept his covert viewings of my little office escapades—flipping off the surveillance cameras, photocopying false memos by the thousands and distributing them via interoffice mail to every state employee in the building, miming "Hey there, Dewey baby!" with pooched lips like I was completely gay. Dewey watched all my greatest hits over and over and over. Kept him amused, I guess. At one time, he'd actually reported the final outcome of his interceptions to Mr. Christ, his boss and the man who'd first hired me, an old guy with horn-rimmed spectacles to match those of his understudy (none other than Dewey) in the analysis of surveillance footage, a damned joke of a job, if you ask me.... *Subject appears to sleep for no less than 1/8 of his 8hr shift. Subject extends middle fingers of both right and left hands indiscriminately until they obscure the camera's view (it is unknown what said subject does for the time the view is blocked)...* I exchanged Dewey's nameplate with Christ's every day for the entire week following the report.

On this final Friday I hung back from his space until my knees stopped quivering. I swaggered up to his cubicle with an unlit cigarette hanging from my mouth. "Hey Dewey, got a light?" He stared up at me through those horn-rimmed glasses the very picture of office propriety: black slacks, oxford buttoned to his neck, black tie. He shook his head. "I don't smoke," he said. So I pulled my lighter out and flicked the cigarette alive. I handed my nameplate to him. "For you," I said, blowing a cloud out over the cubicle next door. Dewey just stared at the plate. I whisked his own from his cubicle wall and put it in my back pocket. I tipped him a good-bye salute, two fingers to my forehead, but before turning away I noticed one of my tapes, a camera seduction, playing silently on his monitor. "My greatest hit, huh," I said.

"The play is rather convincing," he said. He spun a full circle in his chair, ending again facing me. "If I was a chick, I'd go for it." He shrugged. So I tipped him good-bye again and turned to go, but his phone rang. I waited there, watching Dewey nodding to the voice on the phone, grunting his agreement. He hung up after 30 seconds or so and told me it was the Mississippi state police; his mother had been killed. I puffed. Someone back over the maze called out the very obvious fact that this was a nonsmoking office. I puffed again. I couldn't feel a thing. "A man in a cape just jumped," I said. "From the viewing area." Dewey's eyes gazed up uncomprehending, bulging behind the magnification of the lenses. I hadn't a clue what to say to the man. I pulled on the cigarette, holding it there between my lips for what seemed like an eternity. I massaged my temples with each index finger, slowly, closing my eyes to focus on the spot of intense pain welling up back there, to focus it away. It didn't work. So I stubbed out the cigarette on the office's brown carpet, saying "I'm sorry, Dewey. Sorry about your mother," and I left.

On the glass elevator down, woozy from the quick, transparent descent of so many things, I bent my gaze cautiously toward the atrium and saw the man in the cape had likely hit his target, that green cow, the direct middle of the mandala. Paramedics circled around him just next to the sculpture. I flinched, turned quickly away and set my sights on a fat man hunched over his greasy lunch in the back of the food court.

On the train homeward I stood swaying in the fluorescent compartment, hand fighting for control of one of the center chrome poles. My head continued to pound. I decided simply to drink it out, get some advice or just a good ear from A.H., lugged my body into the Two-Way to catch him standing framed behind the bar by the two taps. He nodded when I walked up, stern and serious behind his sunglasses. "Shouldn't you be at work?" he said. The red flames on his tiara shot my way with his head.

"Man I got a headache!" I bellowed. "Gimme a beer. Hey, check it out. I just got fired, man." A.H. did not move to this brash jumble of a proclamation, simply stared on. "And fucking Albert's coming up tomorrow. Good God!" I shook my head. My lately budding jowls flung around like my 30 years had doubled in the very instant. (Premature, just like your grandfather Jeremiah, they all said: Albert, Tope, my crazy father Johnny Jones, all of them: *just like him*.) "What luck!" I hollered through the place.

The old guys at the bar ignored me. Time blew past into night. Empty bottles congregated on the wooden space of the bar in front of me, A.H. refusing to clean my spot until I shut the hell up, so he said, about the two old bastards, about the job, about the headache, but I kept it coming, even diatribes about my wank of a father, whom I'd neither thought a whit about since my brother died, nor seen since I left the state of SC, but whose drunk buddies followed me like a disease, who had my mind going back and back to him. He was a rich headcase, I told A.H. He threw his money around like a particularly unscrupulous patron of the arts, or something, though he never seemed to run out of it. Someday, I would be the recipient of that cash—if the old bastard hadn't blown the load when he kicked off. He got the better of it from his father. Like father like son like…that train of thought didn't get me anywhere I wanted to go, though, and my headache continued to grow. At an uncertain point I found myself complaining about it to this greasy kid who was all done up like an urban cowboy or something. He had a pencil-thin mustache just above his lip and on his feet a pair of short boots, with a little chrome tip at each toe, into which his jeans were tucked. He and A.H. seemed to know each other, yet neither spoke more than a few words, obviously hushed to keep them from the ears of the rest of us. I began telling the boy—not that he was any younger than me—about my alley escapades from the days of yore, when he got excited. "The rat king? Have you ever heard of it? It just happens," he said. "A bunch of fucking rats living in a wall or sewer or whatever get tied together at the tail. They live that way for a while, with fellow vermin helping them out a little, before the brood gets too on the edge, each little fucker starts eating the other, and they end up a bloody heap." The kid looked hard now at me—I was wide-eyed scared, I'll say, picturing this—then burst into laughter.

"Fuck you," I said.

"Hey man, I'm not kidding," he said, then turned back his beer and loudly issued a good-bye, thumping his chest, to A.H., who watched him amble off into the street a little too intently, I thought. "Who the fuck was that?" I said. A.H. didn't answer. "Everything OK?" But he didn't answer that either, and my headache was now verging on migraine status—I just went back to that simple topic.

A.H. said he'd break a bottle over it if I didn't cool it. "That should help the pain," he said. He pointed to my left temple and grabbed the neck of a cold one, swung it around behind the bar. "Goddamn head is killing me," I said to my friend, once more.

His customary phalanx of fat old men hanging heads-down over the bar suddenly perked up, in turn swung their heads around at me, slinging drool and snot over the counter's surface. The men wore cheap grins. This place really got to my last fucking nerve, the gathering of repressed and not-so-repressed queers and, well, A.H., who might look like one of the not-so-repressed variety but for his air of complete indifference. He pulled a wet rag from a sink, wrung it out onto the floor, and, in one quick walk down the length of the bar, wiped the snot of the men clean.

"Damn my head!" I hollered, then standing from my stool and massaging my temples, leaning into the bar just across from A.H. I lifted my bottle, pulling the last from it and slamming the empty down. "Really, really painful," I said, near tears now. The beer was not helping. "Maybe the beers are the cause," I said. So A.H. lifted another bottle, wrapped a toweled fist around its long neck and raised it a foot over his head. I turned from him like I didn't give a damn and tried to focus on the bar-stool men, their greasy hair, the O's on their scratched-up specs which were all aimed my way, their heads nodding slowly at my complaints. The raised red-vinyl forearm of A.H.—best friend, stage actor, musician, theoretician—gave way to his massive black hand, poised high overhead in my periphery and clutching the glistening, twinkling brown glass of the...

Next thing I was flat on my back adjacent a toppled stool, one of the fat men—his frizzed-out hair in enormous silhouette in front of an overhead bulb—slapping me repeatedly, grunting, "Wake up, Bill. Wake up." His hand came away covered in blood. Artichoke Heart's black, cheeky face swung into the picture. "How's that headache?" he said.

I didn't really think he'd do it, I didn't. I tried to tell him as much but I doubt I actually said anything, for he simply smiled and said, "All in good faith, brother. All in good faith."

I woke fully, finally, alone in the hospital, a doctor with an Indian face up above me stitching closed the five-inch gash left by A.H.'s bottle—a parabola around my left temple, the blazing purple end of which you could see, at the terminus of the small procedure, just barely poking from under the monstrous pad and bandage the doctor wrapped around my head like a turban. Orderlies gave me a bagful of antiseptics and clean bandages and cloth tape to hold it all in place. They told me to change the thing at least daily.

"It's going to hurt," I said to the doctor.

"You smell like a drinking man," he said, and it was true: I'd only been here a few hours. I was still drunk. "Drink more," he continued.

A.H. had cured me temporarily, at least, though there and then I silently vowed to make him pay, to exact some kind of revenge, if only for the shame of having to wear that ludicrous bandage for two weeks like a Sikh cabdriver's turban. I got no end of it from Albert and that fatass Tope, who arrived in a cloud at ten the next morning.

They shuffled up through my courtyard, both in flannel shirts with the sleeves ripped out, all four of their fat arms connected to white cardboard cartons full of what I supposed was just a small piece of their stolen treasure. "I just got fired boys," I said, first thing when I opened the door. Tope said that was too bad, cigarette bobbing between his lips. They both dragged on cigarettes without putting down the big cartons, simultaneously shot clouds out over both of my shoulders.

"Yeah," I said, coughing a little. "I just got fired and had to pay the damned hospital bill because the bastards canceled my insurance the very day. You'd figure a bureaucracy like that couldn't get it done in less than a month, but fuck me they did," which was a lie but sounded ornery enough, I thought, to force the matter of their moving on away from here.

"Hell I been fired before," Tope said. The burning tip of his cigarette jumped to his nose, fell back. He pulled hard on it.

"From the bleachery, of all places," Albert said, winking my way, like that would mean very much to me, and laughing a little at his friend.

"Jesus hell," I said. I stared at the space above their heads.

"So what's this about the hospital?" Albert said. "And why you got that dumb-ass-looking-rag on your head?"

"Yeah, looks like them things them Rastafarians wear," Tope said.

"You mean Arabs," I said. "Or Sikhs or whatever. Maybe I've converted." I shot Tope a mean look, my teeth bared, but he missed it completely.

"Yeah, them Rass-tass," he said. "Hell, that means you must have some smoke around here, anyway."

"No smoke, but again: that's A-raabs, pal. Moose-limbs."

"Yeah, Rass-tass." Tope shot a cloud directly into my face. I coughed, a wave of pain radiating through my head and neck. They just stood there, blankly staring, shooting clouds like pros.

I took a few more lines of attack. I talked about the dinginess of my apartment, the lack of space, how Tope would have to sleep in the goddamned closet, really, the place was so small. Then, in the face of their blank stares and jiving silliness, I just gave up, figuring I might as well join the old boys. I lit a smoke and got a little woozy after the second inhale—my head was beginning to really pound, painkillers local and general excreting themselves through all my pores. I wobbled full out into the courtyard with them. "Nice fucking day, ain't it?" I mumbled and sat down, oh so slowly—I'd realized the peril of quick movement earlier when, in the gray haze of half-sleep, I saw the light cover on the ceiling above my bed wiggle a little like it was loose, then come full undone and start on a gravity-propelled trajectory straight for my bandaged forehead. I rolled, launching off the bed just in time, but swooned dizzily into the wall for support after the quick movement.

Albert and Tope sat down either side of me on the stone steps, Tope ripping the top flap off one of the cartons on the way down to reveal a plethora of bottles of Jim Beam, it turned out. Albert leaned over me, gut falling down across my knees, and motioned to Tope to hand him one. "Nice day," Albert said, when finally he had the bottle open in front of him.

"Nice day," Tope echoed.

"Yeah," I said, could think of nothing else. New summer in the city. Sunlight poured down into the west-facing courtyard. Albert brought the neck of the bottle to his cracked lips and pulled, gave a gasp and a loud "Whoo!" and passed it across me to Tope. "Gimme a sip of that?" I said, and Tope got his own long pull, then passed it to me. God bless the doctor: he was right, the whiskey helped. I settled in for the long haul. We sat all day on my little stoop, in the courtyard—we passed the bottle back and forth, we dodged the quizzical expressions and stomping feet of my building mates as they passed in and out of their doors on purposeful ways to the world. When darkness came, I stood, fighting the dizziness and the drunk for a minute or so before wobbling indoors. We stared at the television. The old boys got a kick out of a Queen Latifah show rerun. Albert figured aloud that it gave the niggers something to do. At a loss for some protest, for anything to say, really, I laughed with them. My head—reeling with the drinking and the slight weight of the bandage—felt all the better for it. When your best friend breaks a beer bottle over your head, get drunk with the old folks and laugh about it. Late into the evening: an infomercial for commemorative videotapes of *Dean Martin's Celebrity Roast* blared from the television, the only light now in my little box of an apartment; we lay sprawled drunk three abreast on the foot-deep pile of black corduroy and white T-shirts on my floor. Albert said something about coming up here to tell me something. I looked over at him and struggled to move my lips to ask him what the hell he was talking about. Must have come out wrong, for the two of them just laughed. Last thing I remembered of the night was Tope's big fat body in partial silhouette against the flickering tube, laughter deep and loud, bending down to pick me up, saying "All right, you drunk little Rasteefury—"

I woke the next morning in a comprehensive darkness, atop another pile of corduroy on the floor of my closet. I couldn't raise my head—the left temple pounded. My legs were splayed up above me along the wall like phantoms. My fingertips shuttled to the spot where the pain in my head burned and bleeped most and came away wet. My bandages were gone. I licked the wetness from a finger and tasted blood.

Albert and Tope were awake. The TV blared away on the other side of the closet door tuned to what sounded like the live broadcast of a particularly magnanimous preacher, who went on about humanity's descent, its inheritance of hell and high water. Then he went off on a tangent about women who dressed up too much when they went to church; naturally, they were devils. A little light seeped into the closet through the crack between the door and the floor, though the pile of clothes eclipsed most of it. I struggled to sit up. My legs were numb, no pins and needles even. I tried to will the blood to flow only so much as my brain could actually work over the pounding that coursed through my head. With both hands I kneaded the flesh of my right thigh. The old boys must have heard me in there, amazingly, considering the loud television, for the closet door suddenly flung open, harsh morning sunlight pouring in and sending a spike through the back of my brain that triggered a burst of vomit. "Shit," I gurgled, the raw whiskey-vomit dripping from my chin, splattering down along my chest. I slit my eyes to Tope's bright silhouette above me. "Albert's got something to tell you, buddy," he said, benevolent and dark and kind in the new morning.

"I can't move my goddamned legs," I said.

"We'll get you cleaned up. You'll wanna rebandage that head like

I told you last night," Tope said. I didn't have the foggiest notion of what he was talking about, barely heard him through the screaming pain behind my tightly closed eyelids.

"Why'd you put me in the fucking closet?" I mumbled, but he didn't pay it any mind. He bent double and put his meaty claws in my armpits and hoisted me softly, dragging me out, my dead legs following in a slide along the floor to my little blue chaise. He propped me up in it. My neck was damn near numb too—my head lolled to my right shoulder all on its own. My legs felt foreign laid out in front of me on the chaise. "Goddamnit, get me a glass of water," I moaned, still staring down at my legs and thinking very hard about blood flow, willing pins and needles, at the very least, into them. But then I heard, above the sound of Tope rooting around through my bag of medical supplies, the booming voice of another, saying, "Now, Billy. There's a reason we came," and it was bigger than I remembered or had ever imagined Mr. Albert's was or could be. I struggled to raise my head to his face, turned my eyes to the floor by the chaise, devoid now of all my dirty old corduroys and Hanes tees, followed the grain of that polished, clean wooden plane all the way to my little desk and, sure enough, there sat Albert in a white T-shirt and dark blue jeans. He looked down his fat nose at me. My head just lolled back to the side. "We didn't expect to find this kind of a damn mess of you, boy," Albert said. His eyes flashed a deep, mean thing at me. Tope materialized with a wet paper towel and wiped the stray vomit from my face. My head fell further to the right, though my eyes remained quite locked with Albert's. And even through the pain, I think I knew then that he had been sent.

Albert brushed his stubbly cheeks with his right hand and went on, "And me and Tope here—unfortunately, some say—we've a high-flown tendency to be just as messy, but we've helped you out you can see by that shiny floor under my brogans there. Tope here's gone clean your face and bandage you up, and I'm not going to so much as prevaricate one single word. All is the God's honest truth, and what that is—your father's on his way here, as we speak. In a week we'll be gone, sure, but we are simply the messengers. He's set to arrive at 2AM next week, Monday, in lead of a kind of cavalry, a convoy, rather, of eight or so stock trailers filled to the brim with high-rotten steer and even a few dairy cow, I've heard tell. Gotta be a damn awful smell, either way. Your daddy will be riding a motorbike, an old Harley Tope sold to him just this spring, see, and which he's carted across hill and valley and all the way across Appalachia to a farm down in south Indiana someplace, driving a herd under the open air along with it. He was on horseback when he told me to come up this way, long time ago. I resisted the first time, but finally I'm here. Your father's a kind man at heart, really, though I know your misgivings well. Your poor brother who was likely drove to his madness and death care of the hotheaded bastard, your mother to her death and that Senator Storm, he's getting along mightily, one would guess, and it don't do a hothead well to watch his nemesis plod right along while he's slinging cow dung at a ranch in Anderson...."

I'd heard about my father's cowboy pretensions over the years, though I'd never guessed the neurosis to be this far along. Albert told over the next hour or so of my father's failed first attempt. What he'd wanted to do: take a herd 500-head strong up from South Carolina and over the Appalachians, Albert said. Two years ago the whole operation broke up, just as it was beginning, in a late-night stampede that left the hills between Greenville and Anderson full of roaming cattle. My crazy rich father, apparently, was to blame, for he wasn't immune to the messiness that consumes the men of our time, its particular manifestation in him a drunkenness that came before all. His top man defected on account of it, Albert told, but this year, Johnny Jones was back neat and, again apparently, for the source of the information—though with booming voice from the mouth of an old, trusted—if unreliable—accomplice to me and mine's lives and deaths—was the same man who'd stolen a liquor truck or lied about stealing a liquor truck to get into my apartment to send word of a proposed father-son reunion. Some news simply has to be delivered firsthand, in person—so typical of their ilk, the good old boys I'd moved to Chicago to escape, at least partly. My crazy father's legacy. He followed my ass around three states before I moved here. I was all the way down in Savannah one weekend with some buddies of mine, back in college. We were at this dive by the coast in a fucking ghetto, really. I got into a conversation at the bar with a black man who got paid next to nothing to run drugs in a "borrowed" van from freight ships that came into port there. I was dealing at the time, small stuff, so I could relate, a little. We got to talking about where we came from. I told him up York County, SC, way. "Oh yeah?" he said. "What town?" I told him. "You Jones?" he said. "That's right," I said. "Billy." I'd already told him this three times—and he was drunk, but his eyes now seemed to focus in on something in his head and a big sarcastic smile came across his face. "Your father ain't *the* Johnny Jones, is it?" Me and my buddies ended up getting kicked out after I got into a fight. Seems the man felt he was owed something by my father, who'd apparently spent some time running drugs out of Savannah himself, a little farther up the ladder, as it were, but still—all this cattle-driving business sounded exorbitant even for him.

"It's all over the local papers wherever he passes," Albert said. "But he don't tell none of them what he told me: what he wants to do, see, is set forth an immense whirlwind in this fine city of yours, here in the north, land of the old enemy of the Southern people and the deserters, where the Jones seed has chosen to manifest itself, where you, little Bill, have chosen to desert, which might sound like a joke to you, but your father feels that it is—how do I put it?—imperative that a reconciliation take place between yourself and he and, well, the enemy that is here is nothing but a great kind of neutralizer, as he sees it. A place he's got old problems with, maybe, but not any problem preemptive of his feelings about his own state and your own, you see. Desertion does not have to be absolute, you know. It can be a kind of gathering, a rest and building of strength for the fights of the future. The Confederates knew this. And your father, he contends it. He told me himself, and crazy as he may be, it makes some sense. It has to, even to you, I'm guessing." Now Albert smiled sarcastically but quickly resumed his stern gaze when my own face brightened at the possibility of his realization of the absolute insanity of my father.

"How fucking much did he pay you to come up here and tell me this?" I said.

"That's neither here nor there," Albert rose for a moment and intensified the serious, purse-lipped gaze he had going. Then he sat, again, and went on, "Your daddy is a thinking man, you know that. And so it seems the only logical choice for him, who doesn't need the money off the sale of the herd, and him who reads one day not so long ago about Bombay, I think it was, or somewhere, and is quite tantalized I think by the—Hinduistic, is it?—the Indian opinion of the bovine species. He just couldn't get over the picture of mere cows clogging up city roads just by being in the way, their tyranny of lethargy or something." Albert leaned back now in my desk chair proud of his word choice, I think, smiled, and crossed his arms over the top of his gut. He nodded slowly to let the point sink in.

Jones sets chaos into motion on account of educational television? I couldn't help thinking the man saw a 1970s TV program on exotic old Bombay and held that shit in his mind for 20-some years (right next to his old love of westerns like *High Noon* and *Red River*, *True Grit* and the like) and has just now realized some half-cocked boyhood dream of his own. Which was, I guess, what old Albert was telling me exactly.

I still could not pull my head up straight, which I figure probably had my thinking a bit off, but then Tope pulled it up for me and began to swab at the stitched gash with a cotton ball and hydrogen peroxide, which burned like hell, but no way did it take much of my attention away from the spike still in the back of my head. There was a half-full whiskey bottle sitting on my desk by Albert, open and waiting. "Pass it," I said. Albert laughed, drank from the bottle himself, but passed it soon enough. "You're a damned sight," he said as I pulled, pins and needles finally jumping in my legs as if in reaction to the stuff.

"So I've been told," I said. It brought A.H. to mind. It was Sunday. A.H. had told me something about Sunday that fateful night at the bar. A show? A rendezvous of some sort? I couldn't remember. Every moment from the past week, every moment before the bottle fell on my head, clanged against the next in my mind. Being drunk every day wipes the slate of your immediate past not clean, but like the nasty rags of the men outside the car wash, it leaves an oily and gritty film over any possible recollection. The mythos of the previous day becomes the pathos of the next without the assistance of any semblance of foreknowledge, taking the drinker unawares. The caped man sprung into my mind as he was on his way down, arms out, cape extended, now a smile on his face so blissful as to be narcotic as he hung there in the air for what seemed like an eternity before disappearing, down. A chill began at my neck and coursed through the middle of me to the pins sticking into my knees. I drank. Tope, still holding my head upright, began wiping the back of my neck with a cold rag, under my hair, which the doctor had left alone back there, shaving only just above the cut around my temple. I had to look like a fucking freak.

As if cued by the thought, Albert laughed. "What?" I said. The old man didn't say a word, kept laughing. "Fucking what?" I said.

He rose, whacking me on the shoulder on his way to the kitchen. More pain spiked in my head. He waddled back with a new bottle of his own, which he set to drinking, staring at me from my desk chair, slight smirk on his face. I pulled silently on my own bottle. Tope wrapped the gauze around my head. My God, I thought, my God…

THE PHONE RANG AROUND NOON. IT WAS ARTICHOKE Heart.

Albert and Tope and I were thoroughly drunk and in decent spirits by then, my father a memory quickly fading with the morning's pain. I wasn't about to let A.H. get me down. "How you feeling?" he said, straight away. "Pretty good," I said, and he must have heard the drunken lilt in my voice, for he asked me how wasted I was—I lied and told him I was sober as a horny mule. I pulled on my now near-empty bottle slowly, careful not to let the slosh give me away.

Artichoke Heart wasn't a man for apologies. He did what he did for a reason and saw wisdom in not looking back. I learned a bit from him in this regard. Though when he'd moved north again after only a few months back in SC, recruited a new backing band and resumed his local shows, I'd almost lost faith in the particular wisdom of his conviction. His tiara was set in stone, like the rest of his head, I quickly realized. It had all been part of the plan, which he'd kept to himself. Some people need to talk shit out, I know. Not A.H., who says too much of that gets in the way of the thing in itself. Still, I couldn't forgive him for his latest deliberate act, even if he had apologized.

"We're playing downtown this afternoon," he told me. "In the park. I'm headed down now." Which gave me an idea. Tope and Albert watched me from the chaise now, the former with his fat middle finger solidly in his nose, not bothering to remove it even when I looked his way. I didn't mention them to A.H., nodded slowly along with his voice on the line. "Maybe I'll meet you down there," I said. "Be good to get out after all this."

"I'll see you there," he said. It was the best apology he could do, I guess, but it wasn't enough. I turned to Albert and Tope. On account of their having a place to stay here, I figured aloud they owed me a favor. "So I want you to steal my friend's tiara right off the top of his head," I said.

"Steal what?" Tope said. "You mean he's wearing one of them things like you got on your head for real?"

I explained the situation, and they were just drunk enough, I guess, to go for it. So we kept putting back the whiskey, and when 2PM rolled around I changed into a clean white shirt and corduroys and we packed three abreast in Tope's pickup and barreled down the expressway toward the Loop. The festival was the Taste of Chicago, the biggest of the city's downtown parties, and the oddest for Artichoke Heart to be playing. Put him on the stage at the blues or jazz fests, and his trio of accordions could fit right in, I figure. Put him on at the Puerto Rican Independence Day parade and fest with all his Latin-jive tunes. But the Taste was a food fest and every fat suburban couple in all of Chicagoland made it down for the weeklong endeavor. I guess A.H. had moved "up" in the world. I'd met him years earlier of course at our neighborhood's half-assed version of the same, where men over smoky grills fried up chorizo and gyros and swatted at their pesky kids pulling the hairs out of their legs in boredom while the men attempted to hock their wares off to the 15 people who might have been milling about the square. A.H. had a presence, though, and an outrageously large following. Still, I figured it weren't but a thing for two overweight drunks from South Carolina to steal his tiara and make a clean getaway.

Tope banged the truck up the off-ramp and onto Jackson. My head felt fine the whole rough ride. I prized my flask from my belt and pulled on it, came damn near to crying at the pleasure of it, the sweet, fiery liquid coursing through my gullet. The two old men on either side of me screwed up their eyes to the tops of the skyscrapers. "Damn," Albert said. "Seems like this is a little nicer than your neighborhood. Why don't you get you a place down here?" I didn't bother answering him.

Rather than put Artichoke Heart in the main-stage band shell, they'd built a stage for him and a few other acts just south of the big fountain in a grassy clearing. His big vinyl sign hung up over the top of it, screaming his name in the familiarly devilish, loopy lettering. Albert, Tope, and I hung by the fountain, the old boys staring off west into the buildings like there might have been some answer to their respective plights within the misleading certainty of the city's design. This is what I was thinking, anyway. They were a ragged couple—the skin of their cheeks puckered and permanently flushed by years of boozing it up, like for the past decade, once a day, each of them had taken a meat tenderizer to his own face. I was reminded then by a sharp pain, a boom at my temple, of my own degraded condition. I pulled from my flask. Sweat popped out on my forehead in the sunlight as I watched the slack-jawed men—white undershirts stained at the armpits, blue jeans, scuffed black brogans. If only they were wearing corduroy, I thought. Then, just maybe, I was looking at myself.

A.H. didn't go on for another hour. He greeted me only briefly in the crowd while we waited. "Nice rag," he said, stone-faced, pointing to my head. I nodded. Albert and Tope stood perhaps 20 feet on, talking now together like they'd found an answer in the city's architecture.

A.H. muttered about the holdup. Seems a storm was on its way and a committee in an office somewhere had decided to hold the show, but now the squall looked to be veering northward up out of the flatlands and into the Wisconsin hills. "Sorry for the wait," A.H. said.

"It's good," I said. "I'm in for the haul. Got nothing else to do, you know." I tipped my flask to him and smiled a little sarcastically. "All in good faith, man."

He scowled, but I turned up the corners of my mouth for him and he laughed as if on cue, the son of a bitch. I drank, feeling like a puppet master for once, a role I rarely played with this man. The tiara was there on his head, gleaming. The loose crowd around us seemed to shift like an amoeba with every adjustment of our focus before A.H. walked away. He was near a damned god to some. The crowd around me was all straight from the neighborhoods, downtown for an afternoon fest featuring one of their own, A.H. representing some muddled, gritty-Chicago mini diaspora. Over the heads and raised fists of this inscrutable, motley crew, after the typically electric performance was over, I watched Tope and Albert struggle through the horde up front to take their positions just right of the stage. I waited. A.H. seemed not to want to come out this time. Normally, he launched into the crowd from the stage, and folks would cover him with flowers and even go so far as to lift the man high above their heads on a wave of ecstatic energy. This time, after a good ten minutes of waiting, the hangers-on began to disperse. I inched closer to the stage, swaying with the liquor. My flask was empty. A tight knot of devotees of all shapes and sizes hung on up front, Tope and Albert among them. I breathed, a Herculean effort. I hobbled to within 20 feet of the knot, and here he came, A.H., spilling with his band from the right of the stage and into the little crowd of people, which expanded to make room. A cacophonous scream rose. I lost sight of him for a moment, lost Tope and Albert too, but then his tiara rose from the scuffling of bodies, glinting at its edges in the sunlight. The people lifted him higher. Atop the crowd, A.H. raised his head and caught my eye. I shuddered, turned and looked back to the hulking skyscrapers, pitching back in the same motion a phantom draught from my empty flask. When I gazed back to the little crowd, A.H. had let his head fall back and was being carried out into the park.

Then, big 6'3" Tope shot his fleshy paw way up above the hands supporting the hero's back and grabbed at the tiara. Artichoke Heart's entire body moved with the thing as Tope pulled, tiara stuck hard to A.H.'s head. The slow progression of the crowd stopped. People held A.H. up, strong, though they seemed to be debating what to do. People shouted obscenities at Tope, who had not let go of the flame design. His own mouth was moving as well, but I couldn't make out what he was saying. And then it broke free, a big chunk of A.H.'s wiry black hair pulling right away with it. And Albert and Tope, tiara shoved under his shirt, sprung away from the group with an outrageous quickness, considering their age and drunkenness. They fled into the crowd of tasters among the food booths across from the stage, only a few of the knot around A.H. bothering to speed off after the boys. The rest of the adoring crowd preferred simply to crowd around its fallen hero. I worked up through the knot and into the center, where A.H. sat quite calmly motioning folks to back away with one hand, the other stuck to the left side of his head, from which his hair had been yanked. He caught my eye. I feigned concern, all the while figuring—from the absolutely empty look on his face—that he'd divined my part in this from the first pull of Tope's fingers on the aluminum flames.

But he didn't say it. "You all right?" I said.

"I'll need stitches," he said. "I'm going to need to go to the hospital to fix this shit." All in good faith, essentially. I let my hand rise to my own bandaged head as I backed away.

IN THE DAYS THAT FOLLOWED, TOPE AND ALBERT left town and I shoved the tiara under the Confederate graycoat in my top drawer. I sat indoors and drank whiskey, watched war play itself out on the television and thought about my own few aggressive acts—violence begat itself, and not much more than that. By that time the congressmen and warrior president had already talked about and then set to destroying the country of Iraq. Thorpe Storm had been silent through it all. He was dying, so hobbled now he rarely even got in on a vote in the evenly divided Senate, thus he was again something of a liability to his party. Maybe it was high time for another of his patented party switcheroos. It'd be a great accomplishment for the old bastard, one that might have well represented the irascible pluck of his home state, even if he hadn't the presence of mind to know what he was doing. But yes, I guessed his end was near, and sure enough, the announcement came later midweek from the wing of the military hospital at Fort Jackson in Columbia dedicated to keeping him alive. The representative of the hospital, a woman in a business outfit and military beret, seemed happy it was over. It was a short interview; the northern press, I figured, couldn't have cared much less. More prominent on this day was a Supreme Court smackdown of a severely antiquated state sodomy law. Texas, no less. The president didn't say a word about it, but the reporters seemed to want to interpret his wry grin at the pronouncement as proof of his queerness—they never said it, but they were really searching for shit on the guy in spite of his lies. He enjoyed the support of every redneck in the country. The wussy reporters were shaking in their boots.

On the Web, Rapture nuts were seeing the court's ruling as the work of the Antichrist, of course, likewise the UN's opposition to every military move of the United States, which would be to say nothing of a similar opposition from all corners of the globe. I tried to laugh it off but couldn't really commit to the hilarity. Johnny Jones was on his way to Chicago with a herd of cattle in tow; if that didn't qualify as a prophetic event, I'd be hard-pressed to come up with something better.

A.H. did his damnedest to absolve me of any guilt I may have felt in the theft of his headgear. "We have things that happen to us," he said, when I saw him two nights later behind the Two-Way bar. We stood on opposite sides of the short wooden gulf; I was methodically raising a cigarette to my lips, staring into my reflection: A.H. had gotten himself a big turban of a bandage further enshrouded by a white cloth. It shined bright around the dark skin at the crown of his forehead.

"All in good faith, brother," he said, sliding a sweaty bottle my way. I was beholden to A.H. for my booze. I had no money, having blown the better part of my last paycheck in the two days after Tope and Albert left and the single bottle of Beam they'd donated to my cause had quickly been drained. I grabbed the beer from the counter and pulled. My head had been pounding for three days. I didn't mention it to the reflection across the bar from me, sans tiara and mirrored sunglasses. God bless the man. "All in good faith," he repeated, waving off the two dimes I tried to give him.

I was attempting to make up the routine minus my job, now, but passed out in front of my computer screen without typing a word this night. I crawled some time in the AM, over an only half-renewed pile of T-shirts and corduroy pants on the floor, into my bed.

A knock came at the door not so long later, rapping twice, though softly, so that being awakened I wasn't quite sure if it was real or not. But then someone's hand caressed the wood of the door to my little hole of an apartment once more, and I rose and strode across the room in my underwear and head bandage. I pulled back the door. Elsa stood there. Her lips pressed tightly together and turned up a little at the corners. She wore a white T-shirt and black leather jeans, carried a yellow suitcase, and that was it.

"Billy," she said. She walked in and sat her suitcase on the chaise. She placed herself beside it in the near darkness.

I trembled in the half light of early morning and dressed and she told me she'd been in Berlin, she couldn't stand it anymore, shacked up with a man named Dieter who wrote poetry and drank like a cliché, she said, and she laughed and I laughed a little and clutched at the side of my head at the pain of it. She laughed too, now, again, asking for the first time about the state of my head. "Well," I said. "You'll of course remember Artichoke Heart." Elsa couldn't believe he'd done it, though I left my retaliation out of the story. "Quite a week you've had, poor man," she said, though she was laughing through it all, and I then stood up from the desk chair and, the truth is, I did not crash into her and we did not make love like deranged bats, rusty at the long gone interval, the time—Elsa smiled and said it was good to be back and went on and told me she had work here, a little. The following two days were a haze of her face in my bathroom mirror, her body beside me on my bed but cold, unnecessary, as the days ahead drew themselves in my imagination with cataclysmic importance. A short two days in and Elsa operated with a consistency reserved for, I could only figure, someone with a holy and glorious purpose in this world. On the third, Friday, she woke promptly at 8AM, threw on a T-shirt, a pair of jeans, slung a variety of bags of camera equipment over her shoulder and blew me a sarcastic kiss from the doorway, flinging her head back and smiling before disappearing down the walk.

SATURDAY NIGHT, I CALLED DOWN TO THE TWO-WAY to find that A.H. wouldn't be in until the following day at noon. I called his home and he wasn't there either. But Elsa and I went out nonetheless, sat in the booth cut up next to and under the edge of the bar, one we'd occupied years ago time and again. We drank and stared at one another, myself still quite baffled by her sudden appearance, left breathless again in this bar with the old men and hipsters and other casualties of the forced camaraderie of alcohol, all these shifty temperaments. Like my own, again. "So maybe I'll work in a factory," I said.

Elsa did not respond, just let her gaze settle on my nervous eyes. We talked of nothing, essentially, an obscure book by a less obscure, but quite dead, Russian futurist.

"A factory," I said. "I'm thinking I'll join a union, maybe get into the electroplating business. What do you think?"

"Doesn't sound like a good idea," she said, smiling.

"How about injecto— Injection molding?"

"Strike against."

"Cookies. There's a chocolate factory down Milwaukee Avenue."

"That's a little sweeter."

And I couldn't help but be wooed all over again by the woman in front of me. Though my mind dwelled on nights like this from a different union—far, far away from anything in the ever-present. Suddenly, Elsa jumped up and made her way to the bar for a fresh round of beers.

I downed the last of the one in front of me, closing my eyes against the weak bite of the cheap swill, and, upon opening them...*and lo, I looked upon the deep*...there was Artichoke Heart, seated across from me in a get-up like that of a royal Saudi, the bandage on his head and these flowing white summer robes and things. "Hey," he said, "people just don't like this look so much, but they don't know it's me yet, I think. Though I'd say give the fuckers a few days and they'll profess their love to all the sons of Allah if the pervs can get over devising ways to bring on the Rapture." The focus of the entire bar had shifted to the white-robed black man at William Harmony Jones's table. A.H. saw my brief look of pure amazement, eyes fuzzy and aimed into the crowded void of the place this evening, and he let fly a big belly-laugh, which caught on quickly. I burst, and my own hands flew to my head, which pounded with every guffaw. I gazed up through tears, and A.H. clutched his own cranial injury as well. Elsa walked up behind him amazed to be seeing, it seemed, a threat there in the seat across from me, but I couldn't get anything through the raging laughter now coursing through me, and A.H. across from me, whose left cheek pressed down into the tabletop as he cried in pain and hilarity and more, yes, more than anyone could ever explain.

Elsa had the beers, though, and, setting them now on the table for the two of us, she finally cased the identity of our white-robed friend, big sweet smile lighting up her face and A.H.'s eyes collapsing in a flutter of white before opening full again. The two embraced. And I laughed to myself, thinking of the tiara in the drawer back at my place, the insane picture of Albert and Tope disheveled and drunk among the greater-Chicago public. I felt little regret: A.H. now had the idea. Over the course of the evening, he'd tell us of his great revelation, a thing that said, now, ours was a time for such distinction. His stage show would become a one-man, that of himself in this getup clucking on about how damned tasty were his mama's watermelons and the generally spectacular quality of the fried chicken at Mammy & Sambo's outside of New Orleans or down on 53rd Street. "We'll see how the fuckers like that," he said. I said there's doubtful much cash in it. A.H. fluffed up his robes with his hands. "We'll see, indeed," he said and flashed a smile in the bar darkness, laughing that gargantuan belly-laugh again. He was headed out on an improvised tour, opening act to a local hip-hop duo, that would take him down the east coast—he'd even set up a show in his native Charleston. "You're gonna miss my crazy father," I said. "But tell Charlie and everybody I said hey."

We ordered round after round after round, and toward the end of it, as Elsa waited at the bar, Artichoke Heart grabbed my arm and whispered just loud enough for me to hear, "Listen, man. I want— I want you to call my brother Charlie and tell him if anything happens to me and you hear about it, all right?" On the heels of the laughter he looked like he might be joking, but he slid a piece of paper across the table, which I pocketed. "OK?" he said. I started to speak, to ask him what was up, but Elsa came back and A.H.'s stern gaze lifted and he smiled, winking my way as he welcomed the lady to his side of the booth. I thought later that he was just taking unnecessary precautions, a version of his typical rhetorical flourish. Things can happen out there, I could hear him saying mock-serious as all hell. But this would be our last round, and as last rounds go, it was one for the times.

> 2:02AM: the great Artichoke Heart having commanded you and your former lover to get your shit on, at least once more for posterity, stumble into apartment, lady E. in tow, and collapse onto the floor with her—the bare floor, minus corduroy and white cotton-weave shoved under the chaise in haste. Scab your knees for the first in a long, long time to match your busted head.
> 3:??: dream of diamonds sparkling in a colorless void, raw steaks, and E.J. Pinkerton yet again the bluesman with the head of a chicken now wailing a current of sound, no vagary, no words, just sound. Wake it up, my friend, wake it…
> 4:27: blast from under your covers and to-nite lover into the bathroom. Sway a steady stream of piss around the rim of your commode. Shit. Wipe up the mess and stumble back undercover, sound asleep, and on and on and…

If it all ended right there, this would be a portrait of the most senselessly elated man on the planet. But there was the matter of my father, which I had managed to put aside those few days. Sunday morning he loomed in the back my fractured mind, pushing just ahead of the hangover spike that drove itself familiarly into the base of my skull. I stared into the ceiling, eyes locked on the murderous light fixture. Elsa slept peacefully next to me into the afternoon as I attempted to think my way through the next day.

I didn't get very far conjuring the picture of Johnny Jones in a cowboy hat and atop a motorcycle or horse, the sight quickly disintegrating to become the confines of my apartment invaded by rats or by the surely scurrilous crew he'd have with him: a cavalcade of drunks in jeans and tennis shoes and with vigilante nooses for any who might get in the way. A bad set, surely, though they were just vague shapes in my mind. My apartment was only so big. It may have fit Albert and Tope for a time, but there was not an entire state big enough for both myself and Pop.

Elsa woke and I told her about it, about him, truly, for the first time, how the crazy son of a bitch had a fucked-up design, how, though I'd gotten away for a time, that design appeared to again involve me. I told her of Albert and Tope, and at one point late in the afternoon, the sun drawing down over the western horizon and its light filtering in through the cracked blinds in shelves, rippling silvery through the cigarette smoke we breathed, sitting on the bed, I even pulled from my top drawer the battered tiara and placed it in her hand. She ran her finger over its red surface and looked as if she were about to hit me or begin a tirade which would end with either of our exits. But she did none of that. She lay back on the bed and stared into the ceiling, beautiful as ever in the late light, and then she smiled, dropping the tiara to the floor and laughing hysterically. "It's all a big fuck-up, no?" I said, throwing her a thickly caricatured South. "A big and damned caterwauling fuck-up the likes of which Jesus would not approve, no no." And I had her, yes, and she had me, in stitches, laughing each of us now until we cried.

At midnight we ventured east along the boulevard from the square on a long walk to Halsted, where we picked up a bus heading south. By 1AM we were right downtown and still bouncing toward the edge of Back of the Yards, a neighborhood bordering the old Chicago stockyards, where Albert had prophesied the coming of Johnny Jones to a vacant series of blocks. Elsa had fallen asleep on my shoulder. The city was dark, though the freeway was jammed; from the bus I saw for a passing moment through a corridor straight down a freeway into the unreality of downtown, where even this late humans lined their cars up beaming headlights one after the other in a mindless procession.

Fifteen minutes later, we stood in a cool wind staring east along a wide and empty avenue. "What do you think?" Elsa was saying, sleepy-eyed, but here. I merely pointed into the distance where, out of the darkness, shone a single light, a big Harley blazing this way and, as predicted, at its back a tractor-trailer unit. As the convoy approached, numerous other units were revealed, seven in all, trundling down the city street with my father at the lead. At the stoplight across from us he waved and tipped his cowboy hat. "He's nuts," I muttered, heart wildly aflutter. The light changed, and here Johnny Jones rolled, with a great Harley roar veering left down Halsted with the troops at his back, big machines and containers lining the street in their succession of seven as he stopped a block down, men stepping from the cabs, dirty men with the wild hair and dirty jeans that had so loomed in my mind, some with jackboots, others still even with the cowboy variety and spurs. The stock trailers exuded a stench that reached our nostrils just at the moment my father came walking back up the street toward the two of us. The rear doors swung open, ramps came down, beasts ambled out into the street, onto the sidewalk and from there into the little field here. Elsa muttered something, nudging my ribs, muttering further about how they were letting them out, can you believe it? But my eyes had fixed on the man coming up the walk—unbelievable intensity. I pulled at the arms of my T-shirt. Elsa stepped back from me and was gone from my mind. Johnny Jones came on in a slow swagger. He was smiling, and I couldn't summon a smile to my own face, felt now a little rush of anger that I bit back with my front teeth and lower lip. "Howdy," he said, now ten yards off, and then burst into laughter and skipped up the walk and took me into his arms, where I could do nothing if not cry. My eyes poured tears down onto the man's shoulder, my crazy father, who, as if cued, then took me by the shoulders and held me at arm's length. "Cut that shit out," he said, tight-lipped. And I obeyed, quite like a dog. "Nice hat," he said, motioning up to my now-seemingly-permanent headgear, but he did not go on.

"Tell me about it," I muttered.

"Have you heard the news?" he said. I pursed my lips, wiped my eyes clear. "What news?" I said, looking away, forgetting my own favorite greeting. He grinned, positively beaming at whatever thought was up there. And I dared to look past the mottled gray stubble drawn up with the wrinkles of a smile and into his eyes, a devilishly curious quality there in the brown irises, unbelievably his in the darkness out here: and all shining as if lit by a ghost down by his feet on the sidewalk. I looked quickly away and did not think of my dead brother and long-passed mother. I reached to my side, where Elsa had been. "Don't worry," he said as I started, spun around to find her standing with a dirty bastard clad in scuffed black leather, like Johnny Ramone or James Dean, hair cut up in a little peacock quiff just like Dean, actually. "She's all right,"

Johnny said. "Corey's a mean shit, but he is that, shit. Don't worry," he repeated.

"We're not together, not really," I said. I pulled my flask from my hip pocket and took a big pull. Johnny Jones then did the same, pulling from some invisible pocket in his brown vest an old thing decorated with etched vines and looking quite like it was of the age of some drunk Confederate. And he smiled, again.

"Goddamn, Johnny Jones," I said. At his back, cows were being allowed to mill about the empty lot, overflowing into the streets and up alleys, and the racket was growing. One ambled up to Johnny's side, chewing.

I pulled again from the flask. "Her name's Elsa," I said.

"Pretty name," he said, repeating, "pretty name. Where's she from?" He was listening to her voice, back there all rolled *r*s and slippery tones, questioning Corey the shit as to the purpose of this, gawking at the sight of the burgeoning dazzle of cowhide just as much as myself.

I did not answer my father. "This news," I said.

Johnny Jones's dark eyes, so very much like my own, just as blood-shot and fiery, rolled as a spooked mule's. "You thought I'd forgotten," he said, drinking then from the flask, exhaling. "Thorpe Storm is expired." And he laughed a belly-laugh like that of Artichoke Heart, but crisp and mean. My father was an old enemy of Senator Storm, and the story he unfolded placed all culpability for the old man's death on the head of himself as he explained the confluence of plots that involved fucking arsenic, of all things. The beast at Jones's side moved on when he started talking about Thorpe Storm, as if to deny any interest, as did I, as the prattle unfolded, wild and attractive though it was. It's likely the beast did know something of Storm, as apparently she had come from the land of South Carolina—we all knew something of the man after a political career that spanned 80 and some years.

Looking back and forth between Elsa behind me and my progenitor here parked in front of me telling of poisoning the oldest senator ever to serve the nation, a man who had finally decamped from the land of the sane, who appeared to be dropping off a herd of cattle in a neighborhood fit only for stray cats, maybe, I began to think that nothing less than a heart attack would save me, my own or my father's, take your pick, when I heard Elsa back behind me dislodging herself from the greaser, her footsteps pitter-pattering this way. My father slowed his speech to a full halt when she appeared at my side and she smiled that blooming thing at him, which he answered with his own, a grin I remembered him using on waitresses and a nurse once when he had a kidney stone. My mother would have slapped him, it's sure. Elsa introduced herself, pushing her hand into the light that seemed to well up from the earth underneath the man. Jones smiled, tipped his hat. He finally brought her beautifully long hand up to his lips. The man was a cowboy, after all. I looked away. Hides merged in my sight along the edge of the road. I pondered heart attacks, again, Rapture, fully expecting something very large and brutal to happen.

There was nothing.

I suggested we might get on back, that it was nice seeing him out here, took Elsa's arm and bumped my way through the beasts and across the street. A traffic jam had begun, headlights of the multitudes converged on us here at the intersection. My father called through the rock 'n' roll of bells and moos, his voice hardly ringing clear, but clanging with a disturbing clarity all the same, "I know your address—" and I froze to listen, but didn't catch the rest, as at that very moment a Buick Century, punching its way through the crowd of vehicles backed up at the light on Halsted, attempted a right turn and came to a halt with a great roar of horn just ahead of a steer who eyed the driver like he'd just taken a bite out of the beast's balls.

We trundled north from the wreckage that would surely be. I fell asleep with my nose in Elsa's armpit when finally an hour later a bus had made its way around the madness and prized us 30 blocks north already, almost all the way back to the city center. And we rode on, at home, Elsa riding me and then myself hung up over her back and thrusting until my head and heart felt like they would burst. It didn't mean nothing.

I could stand it, sleeping, without the bandage to pad the injury at this point. A few more days and I'd be off it for good. Despite the pain, I was actually healing—hard to believe, really, when I imagined the indefinite state of my liver at this point. And I did not dream this night. I lay awake for hours recasting the image of my father in that absurd ten-gallon, and I'd convinced myself that it had been absolutely nothing, that my heart was set, content at the disruption.

Elsa's alarm buzzed promptly at eight. She rose, showered, dressed, and had her own breakfast of cigarettes and espresso while I nodded on and off at the prick of nicotine at my nose. But through the old haze of half-sleep I heard her yelping and laughing at a certain point. Soon after, she shook me fully awake and went on about the television, the news. I shot upright in the bed and heard quite clearly now the muted quick-clip of a helicopter and the buzz-saw bark of a traffic commentator, "And whoa! look what we have here!" training my sight past Elsa's shoulder to a live, aerial shot of man on horse in the lead of a small group of bovine specimens in a gallop up the Dan Ryan expressway, alive in the dream. I just laughed at first, Elsa hopping up and down in the middle of the room, and we watched as the man Jones made his way over the next half-hour, behind himself the smaller buildings giving way to high-rise projects and glittering skyscrapers, cars lined up like toy trains for miles, full of minions making their ways slowly, but ever more slowly, to desk-drone jobs like my former own, and I couldn't be happier, for the moment, that the television was there, had been dreamed up by whosoever had dreamed it, that I would never go back to my job and probably would never see this man again anywhere but on the television. "He's fucking crazy," I said, sitting on the bed. "But it's beautiful!" Elsa said, her laughter falling off. It was, is. He had himself a little herd of about 15 or so of the beasts sometimes at his back, sometimes up ahead. Every now and again, he'd turn to face the wall of diesel and gasoline fumes and the roar of horn-honks at his back and he'd rope a cow—just for the sport of it, I figured.

Elsa left, beaming regrets, halfway through it, but I watched on, head beginning to pulse with pain, pounding as the blood rose in my veins. The end happened at the city library—the new pomo monstrosity of interior columns and steel gargoyles guarding its flanks against terrorists of all kinds. A small rodeo was held on State Street, involving not only Johnny Jones but men in the garb of clowns, whom I suspected to be his hands. I thought I spotted the mini pompadour of Elsa's greaser jutting out from behind his mask with blooming red nose. Johnny would indeed be arrested, but not before he got in his piece, standing next to the figure of one of the sculpted "Cows on Parade." His hand lay upon the horn of the concrete-and-enamel beast—painted design done up like a film layover in an old slasher flick, streaked bright red. "See the very travesty!" Johnny Jones was saying, "the travesty you have made of the bovine species!" He patted the art-cow's head and then turned to one of his own, a gracious Holstein who stood on the walk in front of the library's display window, nose stuck haughtily into the air. "Now that's an animal," Jones said, and the crowd of gawkers let fly a boom of laughter as he jumped back and up onto his horse, a trio of Chicago riot policeman in polished blue helmets materializing and dragging Johnny Jones away, dragging him away like a dog, that is, until he broke free, and shots rang out, one catching his right foot. Johnny Jones rolled, jumped up and darted, now hobbling, into the traffic on State. From the other side of the street, someone got off a good shot then, catching him in the chest as the camera angle dramatically switched, like the whole thing was being acted, had been scripted, preordained, Johnny Jones falling hard and silent, a beat-up Mercury Topaz screeching to a halt just before crushing him, though it likely wouldn't have mattered. The man was expired.

BUT THEY DIDN'T KILL HIM, AFTER ALL. EIGHT DAYS later, when he was well enough to talk to anyone, much less me, my father gave me his bank account info, wrote a statement, signed it, and told me to take out enough money to maybe bail him out once he was in (for now, Cook County hospital was his guardian, plus a couple bruiser city cops by the door to his room), though he wasn't quite sure how much would be needed or if it'd even be possible, as his lawyer told him that before it was over he could be up on a recently inaugurated terrorism charge for the incident—Johnny didn't trust the lawyer, who was a Yankee and had been appointed, so he needed me to do this. I told him I would, and left quickly. I went downtown to a bank branch and did the deed, leaving with a few grand in cash. It wouldn't be near enough to get him out if it came to that, I knew, but that didn't matter at this point. I'd made my decision.

I rented a blue Pontiac Grand Prix, two-door, felt like Ricky Craven or some other no-name NASCAR Pontiac driver wheeling it up the freeway from the Loop. I went by the Two-Way to show it off to A.H., but remembered he was out on tour and drove on. At home, I waited for Elsa to get back from work. I happened to step out for some cigarettes, and when I got back, she was sitting on my chaise, crying. My first thought was that somehow she'd realized I was leaving, though I hadn't told her, and this was her anguish at the knowledge; more than a little egotistical of me. As it turned out, I wouldn't have to make that call to Charlie.

Elsa told me word had come in that Artichoke Heart was dead, shot during a show at a bar in Charleston. They caught the killer. In fact, the crowd beat him half to death outside the club, as Charlie told it. A.H. had apparently given his brother just the same directive he'd given me. When finally I talked to the kid, I told him I'd be at the memorial service, which would be held midafternoon tomorrow at Sunny Springs Creek AME Zion just outside Charleston, the Jones brothers' childhood church.

What I didn't tell him was that I was already headed back to the Upcountry and that this stopover by the coast wouldn't be too much out of the way at all, that surely A.H. would dig the convenience of it. Elsa and I exchanged our good-byes, nothing too dramatic, of course—a shared tear for our friend, a kiss on the cheek, a hug. She would keep the apartment as long as the lease lasted, or until her visa was up, or after. I didn't care. I told her to throw all my stuff in the alley when she was done with it. Or keep it. It didn't matter.

Eighteen hours later, at the service, I was the only white guy in the place, but that didn't matter either. This was a charitable bunch of Christians. Charlie and I went out and got drunk and I gave him A.H.'s tiara. He laughed and laughed when I told him my tale of revenge, and then the young man began to cry, and I cried, and we were both infinitely embarrassed. I lit a cigarette and turned away from Charlie, who forced a chuckle and lit his own.

A.H.'s death was revenge, apparently, a tit-for-tat strike. He'd been tailed all the way from New York down here, Charlie said, for the right moment, I guess. The killer meant to spare the family the necessity of body transport, maybe. Thus in a way it was an act of charity. Charlie seemed to want to believe it was so. "Art was into some messed-up shit," he said—it was bound to happen sometime. I remembered days gone by, A.H.'s preposterous claims. But Charlie's manner was overall just a little too forthright. The more drinks we had, the less I bought his grief. "Listen, man," I said. "What's up for real? You can tell me." But he just stared on like I was crazy, and arguably I was—when your best friend dies, refuse to accept it at first; make a spectacle of yourself in the process.

It was an oddly chilly night for summer SC. When I bid Charlie adieu, when he went to the bar's back room to join the rest of the improvised postfuneral party, I pulled from the rental's trunk my topcoat, one of the few items I'd brought along. I put it on and drove the three hours home, rode into town on my fifth cup of roadside coffee spinning at the wheel of the Pontiac, hopped-up and at the same time drunk on the familiarity. It'd been five years or more since I'd been back. The interstate on the way in was lit up even this late with a myriad of chain restaurants' signage, a big mall whose parking lot glimmered with lights like a football stadium, but when I rode into the center of town, all was just as I left it.

I strode up the steps onto Albert's front porch laughing at the sight, the ruts in the rail in front of his rocking chair and all. I knocked, and after a short time the door cracked a half-inch, then further, revealing the disheveled man in a T-shirt and rumpled jeans. "You got some of that Beam left?" I said.

"Damn, Billy," he muttered, motioning me in.

I threw my coat in the room where I'd stay for a while. I didn't know how long it'd be, truly. Maybe from this base I'd venture out, a missionary, maybe torch the Dixie flag on that sick monument in Columbia. Maybe I'd just sit here and drink for a while, see where that led. As I was falling asleep I would be transfixed by the window above the bed through which my brother crawled to his eventual death. Maybe I'd disappear through it too, disappear far away into a crowded Chicago street, one of the many anonymous heads. But you'd be able spot the graycoat among the others, the head rising from its tight collar a little unkempt, maybe even so much so as to be alarming. Look for me there in the near future. Do. Maybe even me and A.H., maybe it ain't over. We'll be smiling, I hope.

Albert pulled a fresh bottle and we went out onto the porch, sat adjacent to each other in his porch rocking chairs. It must have been 2AM.

"You see your daddy?" he said.

"Yeah, I did."

"They tell me he's in the hospital."

"I got no strength for his fight, got enough on my own," I said. "Plus I don't give a shit if it don't make sense and don't care where he goes, the son of a bitch. I got no regrets."

He passed me the bottle angrily. "What the fuck are you talking about? I got no regrets either, Goddamnit," he said.

I dropped the bottle into the wooden gulf between us.

"And you keep on believing that," said Albert Ledbetter. "Drink up." And so we did.

ACKNOWLEDGMENTS

Thanks, first and foremost, to my great Tennessee beauty of a wife, Susannah Felts, who makes life wonderful, and in no particular order to the following folks, without whom this book would not have been possible: Randy Albers, Eric Graf, Joe Meno, William Blackmon, Jeff Dills, Beth & Mike Dills, Vincent & Louisa Dills, Geneva Dills, Jim Munroe & Susan Bustos, Mickey & Danielle Hess, Rob Funderburk, Matt & Julie Halpern-Cordell, Kali Davidson, Judy Corbett, Brian Costello, Jonathan and Zach at featherproof, Greg Ellis, Joe Jarvis, Jerome Ludwig, Sam Axelrod, Chris Sundstrom, Will Weikart, Richard Yoo, Anja Kirschner, Theo Cowley, and Jeremy Bacharach.

TODD DILLS was born and reared in Rock Hill, SC, a town in that state's Upcountry not all that distant from the site where the above photo was taken, of Dills and an erstwhile U.S. senator. Dills is the editor and publisher of THE2NDHAND, the Chicago broadsheet and online magazine for new writing he founded in 2000, and in 2004 he edited a best-of collection of work from said zine, ***ALL HANDS ON: A THE2NDHAND Reader*** (Elephant Rock). He is the author of a collection of shorts, *For Weeks Above the Umbrella* (2002), and his fiction and nonfiction have appeared in a variety of publications, including the *Chicago Reader*, where he's on the editorial staff. He holds an MFA from and is a part-time faculty member of Columbia College Chicago's fiction writing department. This is his first novel.

Praise for **ALL HANDS ON** and **THE2NDHAND**:

"**THE2NDHAND** is at the direct center of the underground writing scene in Chicago." —*Chicago Tribune*

"Like placing your ear beside some kind of magical, future radio and listening to the shocking world of the strange and new.... **ALL HANDS ON**, an anthology of new work and old, features the best of the magazine and a look at what may stand as the underground lit world's most interesting contemporary writing." —*Punk Planet*

"**THE2NDHAND** might be a true heartbreaking work of staggering genius, and unlike *McSweeney's*, you might be able to afford this one." —*Clamor*

"**THE2NDHAND** has been the most exciting literary vessel in Chicago, opening a comfortably padded room for the anecdotal fiction writers and the experimental tale-spinners to play together where no one will get hurt. Read through this collection of four years' worth of stories, and you'll see the line between the two isn't as clear as all that. And in the way the strongest species survive, it would seem the cross-pollination that happened over the years has strengthened both sides." —*PopMatters.com*

"Best Lit in Chicago 2001" —*New City Chicago*

"**THE2NDHAND** has ruined my life." —*Rollie St. Bacon, the rock critic*

www.THE2NDHAND.com

ALLHANDSON

A THE2NDHAND Reader * *Edited by Todd Dills*

Introduction by Jim Munroe

An anthology of works published in **THE2NDHAND** (*Chicago's broadsheet and online magazine for new writing*), **ALL HANDS ON** straddles the line separating the traditional and the new, its pages a mini tug-of-war between beautiful, campfire-style storytelling and high-voltage experimentation. Think like a mountain, rock 'n' roll, draw up the itinerary, live, and try it out.

With stories by:

Joe Meno, Jeb Gleason-Allured, Tom Bradley, Amina Cain, Brian Costello, Greg Purcell, Susannah Felts, Paul A. Toth, Stacy Bierlein, Richard Kostelanetz, Mickey Hess, Hunter Kennedy, and many more.